DAYS OF
FURY

TIMES OF TURMOIL

BOOK THREE

DAYS OF
FURY

BY CHAD DAYBELL

spring creek
BOOK COMPANY
Provo, Utah

ISBN 13: 978-0-9960974-5-1
e. 1

Published by:
Spring Creek Book Company
P.O. Box 50355
Provo, Utah 84605-0355

www.springcreekbooks.com

Cover design © Spring Creek Book Company

Printed in the United States of America
Printed on acid-free paper

Author's Note

As you begin reading this third volume of the *Times of Turmoil* series, it will feel as if only a few days have passed in the characters' lives since the end of the second volume.

However, it has been more than two years since I finished writing *Martial Law*. After sending it to press, I immediately began working on this volume, but after I had completed a few chapters, the Spirit said, "*Stop for a time.*" I was surprised, because I felt I had the story all worked out, but I did as I was told.

Soon afterward, I came in contact with a woman named Julie Rowe who had a near-death experience and then came back from the Spirit World to tell about it. A good portion of 2014 was devoted to helping Julie publish her two books *A Greater Tomorrow* and *The Time is Now*. They are important books that encourage us to follow the prophet and to prepare for the very events I describe in this series of novels.

In the past few months I have also helped Hector Sosa publish his book *A Change is Coming*. Hector has the gift of seeing visions of the future, and his detailed descriptions of upcoming events fit well with what Julie was shown in the Spirit World.

If you have enjoyed my novels, you would greatly appreciate what Julie and Hector share in their books.

Chad Daybell
August 2015

THE ENEMY APPROACHES

As this volume opens, the citizens of Salt Lake City are trying to regroup after a major earthquake has damaged the entire valley and caused widespread flooding.

Aaron Shaw has made his way from the National Security Agency's Data Center near the Point of the Mountain to the home of Elder Bushman, an LDS Church leader who Aaron has corresponded with for several months about the NSA's latest spying efforts. They will soon leave Elder Bushman's home and attempt to reach Temple Square.

Meanwhile, Nathan Foster and his new wife Marie have reunited with Marie's mother Carol and Nathan's half-sister Denise at a camp near Wallsburg, Utah. Nathan is aware that all maintenance missionaries have been asked to return to Salt Lake, and the four of them plan to depart Wallsburg soon.

Nathan's father Garrett is in Nevada as part of the United Nations' peacekeeping force that he joined while in California. He is seeing firsthand the negative effects of the Coalition's newly imposed oil embargo on the United States.

The first outward signs of a national economic collapse are being manifested as prices rise and more companies shut down. Major riots and gang warfare are blossoming across the nation. Commerce has essentially ceased, and food and water have become prized commodities.

In Washington, D.C., mobs have continually rallied in front of the U.S. Capitol Building and the White House. The citizens blame the federal government for the crisis. The U.S. president has addressed the nation and has promised that he is doing everything possible to resume the oil shipments, but his words ring hollow.

The leaders of the Coalition nations are watching these developments from afar and intend to provide their U.N. peacekeepers with additional troops. Within days, thousands of Coalition soldiers from several countries will begin to "put things in order" in the United States through any means necessary.

The Coalition knows the time has come to turn up the heat on America. War is on the horizon.

CHAPTER 1

U.N. peacekeeper Garrett Foster stood in front of the main entrance to the CasaBlanca Resort in Mesquite, Nevada. He and another soldier kept their rifles pointed at a crowd of people who were angrily shouting to let them into the building.

"We're starving out here," a woman cried. "We know you've got some food inside!"

The temperature on this early October day was approaching an unseasonably hot 95 degrees. The city's power was out, and the hope of finding an air-conditioned building was merely a dream. Garrett quickly wiped the sweat from his eyes before putting his finger back on the gun's trigger.

Garrett was sickened at the sight of the lifeless bodies of six men and three women lying between him and the crowd. Ten minutes earlier the horde had rushed forward, but he and the other guard had stopped the attackers in their tracks with a burst of gunfire. The corpses now served as a stark reminder to the unruly crowd against trying that tactic again. As the group's hunger increased, though, their courage to rush the building seemed to be growing as well.

Garrett thought of U.N. Commander Klopov's grin at the announcement of the nationwide oil embargo a few days earlier, but even Klopov hadn't anticipated the surge of animalistic panic the news had provoked among the residents of southern Nevada. The people were still rebuilding their lives after a direct hit by the Great Storm, and the bad news about the embargo had pushed many of them over the edge.

The past two days had been a series of unholy, unthinkable events that made Garrett cringe to even think about, and he hadn't slept for more than a couple of hours since then. The U.N. convoy had left Las Vegas the same day as the announcement of the oil embargo. They had intended to reach St. George, Utah by evening, but they soon learned the highway through the Virgin River Gorge had been destroyed by an earthquake. The convoy had no choice but to stop in Mesquite.

When they arrived in Mesquite, the city was still fairly calm, but within hours it was overrun by people who had driven out of Las Vegas to escape the violence that was escalating there. Some people had purposely followed the U.N. convoy, hoping that it would lead them to food and shelter. Others were simply fleeing anywhere else to avoid the chaos that had filled Las Vegas.

At first, Mesquite's casinos, restaurants, and gas stations had tried to be accommodating to the crowds, but they soon ran out of supplies. The people then moved into the city's residential areas asking for help, but they were rebuffed by the citizens. Battles had broken out in the streets, and gunshots still filled the air even as Garrett stood his ground in front of the casino.

Garrett's radio suddenly crackled to life.

"*This is Commander Klopov. Return immediately to your vehicle. We are moving out in ten minutes.*"

The soldier standing beside him gave a glance. "Is he serious? Why would we leave?"

"Because Klopov knows staying here is pointless," Garrett said. "The people are already moving into a 'survival of the fittest' mode. This is going to get really ugly."

The pair moved away from the entrance, and Garrett shouted to the crowd, "Go for it!"

The anxious group hardly hesitated, stepping over the bodies strewn across the casino entrance. It quickly turned into a surge of humanity as dozens of people rushed into the building.

"This is going to end badly for everyone," Garrett said. "I'm glad we're getting out of here."

Garrett and his partner hurried to their transport vehicles in the far corner of the casino's parking lot. The transporters were surrounded by peacekeepers who didn't hesitate to fire shots at any civilians who got too close.

Garrett saw Commander Klopov standing with a few other soldiers near the lead vehicle. The Russian leader motioned for Garrett to come to his side. They had become friends over the past few weeks, and Klopov had come to trust Garrett's advice, especially about traveling through the western United States.

Klopov looked him in the eyes and said, "The Coalition leaders want us to secure the NSA Data Center near Salt Lake before they begin their full-scale invasion in a few days. But I told them the Virgin River Gorge is blocked, and it might take us longer than expected to get there. Do you know another route?"

Garrett remembered a trip he'd taken many years earlier. "Highway 91 could get us to St. George," he said. "It was the main route before I-15 was built. I'm sure the road was damaged by the earthquake, but with our vehicles we should be fine. There's a town up ahead called Littlefield. That's where we can connect with the old highway."

"I trust your judgment," Klopov said. "Let's go."

The U.N. convoy soon departed, and some foolish citizens tried to hitch a ride on the vehicles. Garret averted his eyes as his fellow soldiers fired numerous deadly shots at them until the few remaining survivors got the message and dropped to the ground.

The convoy traveled north on I-15 until they reached Littlefield, where an incredible line of cars blocked the freeway. The traffic jam went all the way to the massive bluff a few miles ahead that contained the impassible Virgin River Gorge. The drivers had simply abandoned their cars and walked back toward Littlefield. Hundreds of exasperated travelers were now loitering in the streets, arguing with each other on how to solve the situation.

The citizens all seemed to spot the U.N. convoy at the same time as it came to a halt at the end of the traffic jam. Garrett clutched his rifle more tightly as the crowds of frustrated people closed in around the convoy. Suddenly Commander Klopov's voice rang out from a large speaker mounted on his vehicle.

"Stay back! We are on a special U.N. mission and cannot be delayed. I repeat, stay back! Anyone who gets in the way will be eliminated."

The people stayed clear as Klopov's lead vehicle cut through the barrow pit, crossed the westbound freeway lanes, then went down a slope onto a frontage road in order to reach Highway 91. Klopov's driver didn't stop for anything, pushing a few cars out of the way as he went, and even crushing a white Geo Metro that was blocking his path.

The other U.N. transporters followed his path and headed north, but as they passed through Littlefield a man jumped onto the side of Klopov's vehicle.

A shot rang out, and the man crumpled to the ground with blood spreading from his lower back. The man screamed out in agony, and Garrett felt sick inside. He was still disturbed by the violent, cold-hearted approach of his fellow "peacekeepers."

The U.N. convoy soon left the hungry masses behind and drove through the night along the highway. They sometimes saw other travelers on the side of the road who had run out of gas. These people would wave frantically as they begged for help, but Klopov didn't even glance at them.

The convoy didn't reach St. George until morning, due to extensive earthquake damage to the road. The city seemed like a ghost town compared to the chaos in Nevada. Garrett guessed that most of the Mormons were long gone, and everyone else was wise enough to stay hidden in their houses.

They got onto St. George Boulevard heading to I-15. Garrett looked for the St. George Temple, because he was afraid the building would attract Klopov's attention. However, it wasn't where it was supposed to be. All he saw was shimmering redrock hills in the distance. The temple should have been clearly visible on the right side of the freeway. He couldn't understand how that magnificent white edifice had disappeared.

Garrett took one more look to the right, and this time to his surprise he could see the temple standing prominently in the center of the city. After a few seconds, it vanished again. His heart burned within him that God had created a mirage to hide the temple from the U.N. convoy.

"I really am on the wrong team," he muttered.

CHAPTER 2

A few hundred miles to the north, Aaron Shaw climbed up onto the large trunk of a fallen tree. He then reached back to help Elder Benjamin Bushman join him. The pair had left Elder Bushman's home on Salt Lake City's east bench two hours earlier in order to reach Temple Square. It was a journey of only a few blocks, but there was so much debris obstructing the roads and sidewalks that their progress had been excruciatingly slow.

As they stood on the tree trunk, they had their first clear view of the downtown area. It was a beautiful day, but the scenery was shocking. Flood waters still flowed through Temple Square's historic buildings, and the devastation caused by the recent earthquake was horrific.

Aaron looked up at the nearby skyscrapers, and every one of them had hundreds of shattered windows. A few of the older buildings had actually pancaked on themselves. Others had partially collapsed or were on the verge of doing so.

Aaron could hardly believe it had been only a few days since he had been driving to work at the NSA Data Center near the Point of the Mountain. It felt more like a month.

"Do you think it's safe to try reaching the temple?" Aaron asked Elder Bushman. "We'd probably have to swim. The water looks fairly deep in most places."

Elder Bushman pointed toward the LDS Conference Center. "Let's work our way along the hill and check there first," he said. "Maybe we'll find someone who can tell us where the other Church leaders are."

Within a few minutes they reached the northern side of the Conference Center and followed a stairway to the roof. Aaron noticed that the earthquake had left the building relatively undamaged. They approached a glass door, but it was locked. Elder Bushman banged on the door several times, but there wasn't any indication someone was going to respond.

Aaron shook his head. "Step back. It feels sacrilegious to do this, but . . ."

He picked up a chunk of broken concrete from a flower bed and hurled it through the door, sending shattered glass everywhere. He then carefully cleared away any remaining glass from the door frame and stepped into the Conference Center. Elder Bushman followed him.

"Hello?" Aaron called out as they inched forward into the building. "Is anybody here?"

"Don't move!" a voice yelled from a dark corner.

Aaron and Elder Bushman instinctively put their hands in the air as a man dressed in dark clothing approached with a flashlight in one hand and a pistol in the other.

"Hey, hold on," Elder Bushman said. "I'm a General Authority of the Church . . ."

"Then why are you throwing rocks through the door?" the man asked.

Aaron cut in. "No one would answer our knocks."

The man shined the light in their faces, then he gave a small laugh and lowered his gun. "Elder Bushman, why didn't you just say your name?"

Elder Bushman breathed a sigh of relief as he recognized the voice. "Bryan, I thought you were stationed in the Church Office Building!"

"I've been doing some part-time security shifts over here," Bryan said. "I was on duty when the earthquake hit, and I've just stayed in the building since then."

The two men warmly shook hands, then Elder Bushman motioned toward Aaron.

"This is my friend Aaron Shaw. He's been working undercover at the NSA Data Center and has some vital information to share with the other Church leaders. Do you know where they are?"

Bryan shook his head. "The Conference Center was empty when the quake hit that morning, and I haven't encountered anyone else in here. I've seen some lights shining in the temple at night, though. You could try there."

Aaron went to a window that had a nice view of the Salt Lake Temple. He saw the water was still lapping against the temple walls. "It looks almost impossible to get in there," he said. "Even if people are inside, I don't think they're going to open the doors."

Bryan looked thoughtful. "There is another option. I wonder if the underground tunnels are flooded. We could give them a try."

❧

A few minutes later the trio had made their way down several staircases to the Conference Center's lowest levels and were now carefully walking along a corridor in calf-deep water.

"The water is calm, rather than rushing like a flood," Bryan said. "So I'm hopeful that means the tunnels are still intact after the earthquake."

He slowly opened a large metal door, and a rush of tepid water poured in that drenched them up to their chests, but then it ebbed away.

Bryan looked back at them. "This passage goes under the street and directly to the temple, so I think we're going to be okay."

They sloshed ahead through the darkness for several more yards, then Bryan opened another door and shined his flashlight around. They realized they'd reached the temple's dressing rooms.

"Good job, Bryan," Elder Bushman said. "We made it."

Bryan shined his flashlight around the room. The wallpaper was damaged nearly to the ceiling. The water was now only up to their knees, but it was clear the area had been completely flooded after the earthquake.

They spotted a staircase, and as they climbed it, they heard an agitated conversation taking place above them. Aaron looked at Elder Bushman and whispered, "What should we do? I don't want to barge into an argument."

"That sounds like Elder Smith of the Quorum of the Twelve," Elder Bushman said. "Let me go ahead of you."

He climbed to the top of the stairs, then called out, "Hello! Elder Smith? It's Elder Bushman of the Quorum of the Seventy!"

The conversation stopped, and a middle-aged man appeared with a gun drawn.

Elder Bushman held up his hands. "Hey! Be careful with that. Didn't I hear Elder Smith's voice?"

The man took a step back. "Are you alone?"

"No I have two men with me down below, but I promise you that we come in peace."

An older man then peeked his head around a doorway and said, "It really is you! Welcome."

The two General Authorities moved toward each other and had a quick embrace.

"I'm glad you're all right," Elder Smith said. He looked toward the stairway and called out, "Come on up."

Bryan and Aaron climbed the stairs and stood next to Elder Bushman. Elder Smith greeted them before saying, "I can't help but wonder how you got in here. I thought we had all the entrances being watched."

"Bryan led us through a tunnel from the Conference Center," Aaron said. "I hope we didn't do anything wrong."

"Not at all," Elder Smith said, but he motioned to his guard. "Have Bryan show you the passage they followed to get here, then secure the doors."

As the two guards went down the stairs, Elder Bushman looked up at the ceiling. "Did the earthquake do much damage to the temple?"

The apostle shrugged. "Oh, some of the chandeliers really swayed, and some fixtures fell, but overall the temple is in remarkable shape compared to the other buildings downtown. The flooding in the lower floors is where the most repair work will need to be done."

"We'll be facing an uphill battle, though," Elder Bushman said. "It took us two hours to get here from my house a few blocks away. It's going to take months to clean things up, especially with the damaged skyscrapers dangling above us. Things might never be normal here again."

"I agree with you," Elder Smith said.

"Where are the members of the First Presidency and the other apostles?" Aaron asked.

Elder Smith shook his head sadly. "The prophet and his counselors are in a safe location, but half of the Quorum of the Twelve were on assignments in other parts of the country when the earthquake hit, and we've only had sporadic contact with them.

The others and myself were here in Utah, but only three of us are accounted for. So we are definitely in disarray, but I'm amazed at how calm the prophet is. I talked to him through the Church network yesterday. We knew these troubles were coming, and we'll be all right. We're prepared for the next phase of the work."

"I want to help you," Aaron said. "I worked at the NSA Data Center until the earthquake hit, and we had been monitoring a U.N. military force that is coming this way from Los Angeles. They were planning to move along I-15 toward Las Vegas even before the earthquake struck here. Since their leaders love to take over disaster zones, they've probably already added Salt Lake as a key destination."

For the first time, Elder Smith seemed a bit alarmed. "That could be serious. What do you know about the giant hole the earthquake caused in the south end of the valley? Did it swallow parts of I-15? Will that stop the U.N. forces?"

"I saw the hole as I traveled here. It is miles across, but they'll be able to get around it. They'll easily reach Temple Square."

Elder Smith nodded grimly. "I need to contact the prophet again tonight to see if it's time to gather to our temporary headquarters.

Until then, you two might as well get cleaned up."

Aaron and Elder Bushman looked at themselves. They were soaked from their journey through the tunnels. The apostle led them to another room where there was additional clothing.

"Before the earthquake, we had been inspired to clean out the lower floors as much as we could," Elder Smith said. "Otherwise everything would have been ruined."

As they were looking through the clothes for the right sizes, Aaron said to Elder Smith, "You're a great inspiration to my daughter's boyfriend Nathan Foster, the missionary who saved your life in Minnesota."

"Oh yes, Elder Foster. What a wonderful young man. How is he doing?"

"I wish I knew," Aaron said. "He went to Chicago to rescue my daughter, and I think he reached her, but I haven't heard from them since."

"Don't worry, they're in the Lord's hands," Elder Smith said. "Nathan has much to accomplish yet."

CHAPTER 3

Nathan Foster kept a firm hold of his mother-in-law Carol Shaw's elbow as they hiked up a steep trail in the foothills above Heber City. Carol was making a valiant effort to reach her ward's camp near Kamas, but her legs were quivering and were nearly ready to give out.

They had been walking for five days and had eaten the last of their supplies that morning. They had discovered a small stream two hours earlier and had refilled their water bottles, but those were now empty. They had expected to reach Kamas by now, but the hike from the Wallsburg camp had taken much longer than they had planned.

"We'll stop at that flat area up ahead," Nathan said as he steadied Carol. "You're doing great."

Nathan's wife Marie and his sister Denise were a few steps ahead of them. Marie turned around and gave her mother a nervous look. "Are you okay?"

"I'm fine," Carol said with a weak smile. "I'll crawl there if I have to."

They soon reached the flat area on the hillside and paused to look across the Heber Valley. The view was amazing yet daunting. The remains of the Jordanelle Reservoir dam could be seen to the north, and the path the torrent of water had taken following the earthquake was clearly visible. Very few structures in the valley had escaped being damaged by the flood.

As the others rested, Nathan walked up the slope to gauge what awaited them. He shook his head as he saw that the remaining journey would be as challenging as the last few miles had been.

Nathan felt his calling as a maintenance missionary weighing upon him. He needed to get to Salt Lake as soon as possible to heed the message he had received in Nauvoo, but he hadn't dared leave his loved ones in the Wallsburg camp. So the morning after their joyful reunion there, he decided to take the others to the Kamas camp where their former Orem ward members were gathered. Nathan had delivered supplies there a few times and knew the route by heart.

He had invited other members of the Wallsburg camp to join them, but there hadn't been any takers. They were content to stay there for the time being.

Nathan had hoped to find some gasoline in Wallsburg and refill the truck that he and Marie had traveled in from the Nauvoo Temple, but he was told the camp's fuel had been used up weeks before to run their portable generators.

So the four of them had begun walking to Kamas, which had created their current dilemma. The hike had actually been very beneficial for Denise, both physically and spiritually. She had been raised in the Catholic faith by her mother Vanessa, but ever since Nathan had come into her life, she had been very intrigued by the teachings of Mormonism.

When they first started hiking, she had fired off several questions. Finally Nathan took the initiative and essentially taught her the missionary discussions as they walked along. Denise had absorbed it all.

"I know what you are teaching me is true," she said on the third day. "I want to become a member of the Church. How can I join?"

"You must be baptized," Nathan had told her. "But it needs to be done in the proper way. We need to reach a camp and have an authorized priesthood leader interview you and approve it."

"I can't wait," Denise had responded.

Nathan snapped out of his memories and looked back toward the others farther down the slope. Marie was watching him.

"How does the trail look?" she called out.

"Not very good," he said. He spotted a small grove of trees about fifty yards ahead and pointed at them.

"Let's meet at those trees," he said. "Once you're settled in there, I'll try to reach the Heber Valley Camp to get help."

&

The grove of trees worked out well as a resting place, and Denise even found a small spring that they could drink from. Nathan refilled his own water bottle and then spent the next hour climbing straight up a ridge where he thought the road to Heber Valley Camp would be. He had guessed right, and he paused to catch his breath as he sat on the pavement. He could barely see the grove of trees a half mile below him.

He stood up to survey his surroundings. He'd made a few deliveries to the camp as a maintenance missionary, and he realized the main entrance was only two more switchbacks away.

Suddenly a dark four-wheeler emerged from the trees on his right. The driver was a middle-aged man wearing camouflage, and he parked the vehicle in the middle of the road facing Nathan.

"Hello there," Nathan called out. "D&C 4:7."

"That's nice to hear, but I need you to follow protocol," the man said. "Do you have anything else to say to me?"

Nathan nodded. "Ask, and ye shall receive; knock, and it shall be opened unto you. Amen."

"That is correct," the man said, acknowledging the Church's password. "May I ask your name?"

"Nathan Foster. I'm a maintenance missionary."

"Nice to meet you. I'm Paul Jackson."

He pulled out a gadget the size of an iPhone and touched a few buttons on the screen.

Nathan gave him a curious look. "I'm guessing you're not trying to connect with Verizon or Sprint."

Paul grinned. "Nope. This is the Church's own network that we got running a few weeks ago. This way we aren't dependent on anybody else. I doubt the government even knows it exists."

"I heard a little about it earlier this year, when I was at the Bishop's Storehouse in Salt Lake," Nathan said. "Is that the network Church leaders can use to find out if family members or friends made it to other camps?"

"Yeah, we've spent the summer getting people registered into the ZOOM system."

"ZOOM?" Nathan asked.

"That's what we call it. It's an acronym for the Zion Official Online Membership database. It lists everyone who is at one of the Church's 'white camps.' We can send messages to each other and verify if people are really who they claim to be. You said your name is Nathan Foster?"

"Yep."

Paul typed in a few words, then said, "You served a mission in Minnesota, and you're a maintenance missionary based out of the Bishop's Central Storehouse."

"Yes, that would be me."

Paul looked at him curiously. "Then what are you doing clear up here?"

Nathan shrugged. "Family reasons. I need your help to get my wife, mother-in-law, and sister to safety. They're waiting at the bottom of this ridge."

"What's their status?" Paul asked. "Are they chipped?"

"Not currently," Nathan said.

Paul raised his eyebrows. "Give me their names. I need to check their status with the government before we bring them to the camp and enter them into the ZOOM database."

"You can do that?"

"Yeah, it's kind of amazing. We've had a guy working undercover in the NSA Data Center who helped us link into their network."

Nathan realized Paul was likely talking about his father-in-law Aaron. "I understand why you need to check who they are," he said. "They are Marie Shaw, Carol Shaw, and Denise Foster, all from Orem."

Paul typed in the names and nodded after each one. Then he smiled. "They are all listed as government fugitives, but hey, who isn't right now? Let's go back to camp and get a couple of more four-wheelers, and we'll pick them up."

"Thank you," Nathan said as he climbed onto the four-wheeler behind Paul. They rode to the main entrance of the Heber Valley Camp and stopped to talk to the guards at the gate.

The guards asked him several questions, and Nathan gave them a detailed explanation why his relatives hadn't gone to the white camps at the time of the prophet's invitation. He also described Aaron's assignment with the NSA.

"I guess that's why you weren't surprised to hear me say a Church member works undercover there," Paul said.

Within minutes Nathan, Paul, and his son Jake were each riding a four-wheeler back down the road. They stopped at the spot Nathan had climbed up the ridge.

"They're in that distant grove of trees," Nathan told the others. "Is there an easier way to reach them?"

Paul studied the slope and said, "The road winds down to within a hundred yards of them on that other ridge. Let's go."

✺

Meanwhile, Marie, Carol, and Denise were resting in the grove. Carol was sleeping soundly on the ground, and Denise was taunting a few red ants with a stick to keep them away from Carol. Marie watched her for a while, but she was starting to worry about Nathan. Then something caught her attention.

"Does that sound like an engine?" she asked Denise.

"Yes. Maybe more than one."

They stood up and peered through the trees. The engines stopped, and to their relief they heard Nathan call their names.

"Hooray! He found help," Marie said, shaking her mother awake. "Mom, we're going to be okay."

Nathan and the two other men soon joined them. "We're in

luck," he said. "This is Paul and Jake. They're going to take us to the camp."

Carol couldn't contain her tears. "Bless you both. I can hardly take another step."

Paul and Jake assisted Carol across the slope to the four-wheelers, where they helped her onto Paul's vehicle. Jake and Denise rode together, while Marie joined Nathan.

Ten minutes later they passed through the camp gate, and Paul led the way to a pavilion. Word had spread that new arrivals were coming, and people wanted to greet them. Nathan recognized Elder Greg Cluff of the First Quorum of the Seventy standing at the front of the group.

They dismounted, and Elder Cluff moved toward Carol. "My dear sister, thank you for your sacrifice. I know your husband Aaron, and he has done so much to help the Church."

"I appreciate that," Carol said. "We're relieved to be here. We were on our way to the Kamas camp when the earthquake struck."

Carol was pleasantly surprised at the difference between the Wallsburg camp and this camp. There were plenty of smiles among the members, and the camp was well-maintained and clean. No one seemed to be hungry, and she could tangibly feel the Spirit of the Lord surrounding them.

"You'll be safe here," Elder Cluff told her.

"I know," Carol said. "I've missed this feeling."

Several of the camp members came up to the newcomers and asked questions about the situation in the cities, but Elder Cluff put a quick stop to it.

"Let's hold off for now," he said. "After they've had time to clean up and eat, we'll meet as a group this evening and invite them share their experiences."

CHAPTER 4

As evening approached in downtown Salt Lake City, Aaron Shaw was feeling restless. Elder Bushman was exhausted from their lengthy hike across eastern Salt Lake earlier in the day, and he was now napping in a side room. The two guards had briefly returned, but they'd left again to check on other tunnels beneath Temple Square.

Elder Smith was keeping an eye on a laptop computer that was being powered by a solar panel on top of the temple. He hadn't heard from his wife since the earthquake and was hoping for any news of her condition.

"I had just arrived here at the temple when the earthquake hit that morning," he said. "Our house is about a mile south of the Bountiful Temple, and our escape plan has always been to go there if anything tragic happens. The temple guards haven't seen her, though. I'm starting to fear the worst."

"Maybe she's helping others," Aaron said hopefully. "From the videos I've seen of you two together, she seems like a go-getter who would worry more about others than herself."

Elder Smith showed a hint of a smile. "You're right. But I wish she would check in. The reports coming in from the maintenance missionaries in Davis County say that most of the homes on the Bountiful hillsides were damaged. In my neighborhood, some houses slid partway down the slope and into the road."

Aaron paused, worried that his next question might be too personal, but he had to ask it.

"May I ask why you and your wife weren't at one of the camps?

20

I know some of the other General Authorities and their spouses have been out of the valley for a while now."

"That's a fair question," Elder Smith said. "Obviously some of the older apostles went to safer places for health reasons. It wasn't an accident that the apostles were scattered across the country when the earthquake happened. The prophet didn't have an exact date given to him about this earthquake, but ever since the first earthquake hit a while ago, we've known the sequence of events that would occur."

"So this earthquake was expected?" Aaron asked.

"Of course," Elder Smith said. "Many of the members have seen it in dreams and visions. We knew that after the Saints had gathered to the camps, this more devastating earthquake would disrupt life here for months to come."

The comment made Aaron bristle a little, but he kept quiet. Elder Smith noticed his sudden change of attitude and said, "Go ahead. Tell me what's on your mind."

Aaron shrugged. "If you knew this earthquake was coming, how come the prophet didn't tell us about it? I just spent a week crossing this valley, and I saw unbelievable problems. Many of those issues could have been averted if the prophet had just been more direct when he issued the invitation to gather."

Elder Smith had heard this argument before, and he understood what Aaron was saying, but it was time for some clarification on the matter.

"A prophet has the difficult task of finding the right balance between knowledge and accountability," Elder Smith said. "For how many years have the prophets been telling the Church members to be prepared for upcoming trials?"

"At least a century, if not longer," Aaron said.

"You're right. You might even say it started with Joseph Smith himself. But the point is the warnings have been given, and for the most part they have gone unheeded."

"That's true."

"So you would have preferred the prophet say, 'I invite you to gather to the camps in the mountains . . . because a huge earthquake is going to destroy your home within a few months.'"

Aaron hesitated. "I see where you're heading with this. Such a statement would make the members fully accountable for how they responded to the prophet's words."

"Correct," Elder Smith said. "The Savior chooses to be more merciful. That's why He and his leaders work in parables. They tell stories in General Conference that have deep meaning for those who are prepared to hear the true message. These Saints 'stay in the boat and hold on,' so to speak. Meanwhile, those who aren't quite ready to respond faithfully will hear the same sermon and come away with a memorable story, but they aren't held to a higher standard."

Aaron saw the wisdom in that route. "There's no doubt the members have been warned many times to get their lives in order and to follow the prophet," he said. "I guess the thousands of people who are in the camps are a testament that they got the message."

"That's right, and the ones who stayed behind have suffered the effects of their choices," Elder Smith said. "This is all part of our learning process here on earth. It hasn't been easy for any of us. Just trust that the Lord is in charge, and He will be more merciful to all of us than we can imagine."

Elder Smith suddenly sat up straight. "You know, you really should see the valley. I know you've seen it from the ground level, but I feel it is important for you to get a good look at it."

"I would like that," Aaron said.

Elder Smith stood and patted Aaron on the back. "Let's go to the roof."

❧

Within five minutes Elder Smith pushed open a door that led to the roof of the Salt Lake Temple. He led Aaron to the northwest spire and pointed out across the valley.

"I think we got water from all types of sources, but the Great

Salt Lake must have tilted this way," Elder Smith said. "Otherwise I don't know how everything could still be so flooded."

Aaron almost felt dizzy as he took in the panoramic view of the downtown area. He looked to the northwest where the apostle had pointed, and the flooding seemed to stretch endlessly.

Aaron could see Antelope Island in the distance, and there wasn't a break in the water between the island and the temple, other than buildings and freeway overpasses jutting out of the water.

"That's bizarre," Aaron said. "Do you know if the lake has flooded everything all the way up the Wasatch Front?"

"Some parts aren't quite as bad, but anything at a lower elevation is submerged. Our reports say the Willard Bay dikes ruptured, and it's basically impossible to get between Ogden and Brigham City because of the flooding."

They turned and looked toward the south end of the valley where the sinkhole was, but they were too far away to see much. Just then three black helicopters came from the north near Ensign Peak and flew low along the foothills toward the University of Utah. The two men instinctively moved behind the temple spire.

"Where are they operating from?" Aaron asked.

"Hill Air Force Base suffered only moderate damage in the quake, and the government is using it as the main base to coordinate the area's relief efforts until the water subsides."

Aaron shook his head. "From what I learned working for the NSA, there's a lot more to it than just helping us out."

"Absolutely," Elder Smith said. "That's why the time has come for the headquarters of the Church to leave Salt Lake. We are leaving guards at the temples here, but the Church's focus is shifting elsewhere."

"Are you talking about New Jerusalem?" Aaron asked.

Elder Smith chuckled. "No, it's not quite time for that, either. Think about it, though. Is there anywhere we've devoted a lot of money and effort for such a seemingly remote place?"

Aaron raised his eyebrows. "BYU-Idaho?"

"Bingo," Elder Smith said. "In the short time since the

earthquake, BYU-Idaho has been transitioning into the temporary headquarters of the Church. For several years we've had everything in place there in regard to communication technology, not to mention a strong base of faithful Saints in Rexburg and the nearby towns. The Church will quietly move forward there and in other gathering places while the nation is cleansed, then we'll regroup and go forth to Missouri to build Zion."

"Wow, I hadn't even considered that before, but it makes perfect sense," Aaron said. "Plus it gets so cold there in the winter that our enemies will stay away."

"Well, that's our hope. The remaining apostles are making their way to Rexburg, and I need to travel there myself. I just really want to know the fate of my wife."

Aaron glanced at the helicopters still circling the valley and said, "I think we better find her before it's too late for all of us."

CHAPTER 5

The four newcomers at the Heber Valley Camp had been given a tent to share. They had bathed, eaten, and had even taken brief naps. Now they were sitting under a pavilion facing a few hundred camp members who were eager to hear their experiences.

Carol smiled at the crowd and noted again the difference in their countenances compared to the inhabitants of the Wallsburg camp. These Saints were filled with light, and they exuded a sense of purpose and confidence. Nathan was nearly overwhelmed by their goodness.

"This is a people that can build Zion," he said to himself.

Elder Cluff picked up a microphone off a table and stood before the crowd.

"Thank you for coming to this impromptu fireside," he said. "We have four new camp members. They are each going to share their experiences of what has happened to them since the day the prophet invited us all to gather. We will begin with a prayer."

An older lady gave a heartfelt prayer, then Nathan volunteered to speak first.

"Hello, my name is Nathan Foster, and I commend you for following the prophet," he said. "I've been serving as a Church maintenance missionary since the spring, and I observed a sifting among the Saints even before the prophet's invitation. People who were active members of the Church just a few months ago are now dead because they chose to disregard the prophet's counsel. Other members are in the so-called 'blue' camps, and their lives aren't pleasant. Earlier this week we were in the camp in Wallsburg, and they are nearly out of food. Many of them are contemplating going back into Utah Valley, which would be a terrible decision."

A man in the front row raised his hand. "Can you give us some details about what is happening across the nation?"

"Yes. Marie has recently been living in Chicago, and she can tell us more about that, but there has been major destruction. The Great Storm swept all across the nation. We were in a camp in Illinois when it hit, and it destroyed everything in its path. Gardens were smashed by the hail, and buildings were damaged. Then came the Black Flu. Marie caught it, and she looked like a corpse. Her body was turning black and was covered with oozing sores, but through the mercy of the Lord, I was able to give her a priesthood blessing and heal her."

The audience murmured their amazement as they gazed at Marie. As everyone quieted down again, a man asked, "So has the economy completely crashed?"

"It has. Money is essentially worthless now, and people are getting desperate. Anyway, I want to let the others talk, but I assure you with all of my heart that coming to this camp was the wisest decision you have ever made."

Nathan then turned and handed the microphone to Marie. She stood before the group and couldn't contain her emotions. She cried for nearly a minute, and Nathan started to get up to assist her, but she waved him back.

"Sorry about that," she said, "but I guess you could say I'm the Prodigal Daughter of this group. My name is Marie Foster, and I should have been dead five times over in the past few months, all because of pride and seeking the things of the world. Nathan and my parents could sense what was coming, and they tried to warn me earlier this year, but I thought they were crazy. Actually, that's wrong. Deep down I knew they were right, but that would mean all of my plans and goals were going to be dashed. So I accepted an internship in Chicago."

A woman called out, "Did you get the chip?"

Marie held up her right hand. "I did, and now I have a jagged scar for the rest of my life from when Nathan helped slice it out."

"Hey, I did the best I could under the circumstances," he said, and the crowd chuckled.

"He was as gentle as possible," Marie said. "The stupid thing is easy to implant, but it is no fun digging it out. Anyway, while I was there, the Black Flu sent everyone into a panic, and almost overnight Chicago became a war zone. I was blessed to find a place to hide, and for a week I cowered in fear as I heard shouting and commotions going on all around me. I was nearly out of food and water, though, and I had accepted that I was going to die. Then miraculously Nathan came all the way from Utah to save me. I don't have time to go into all of those details, but we eventually made our way out of Chicago, although we nearly got caught by a government agent who had tracked my chip. That's when we removed it."

Nathan spoke up. "As we were leaving Chicago, a huge fire was engulfing the city. Those magnificent skyscrapers were going up in flames."

"It was horrific," Marie added. "We walked for several days before being taken in by a Baptist group. That's who we were with when the Great Storm hit, and when I was healed from the Black Flu. Then we felt prompted to travel to Nauvoo. We thought it might be a gathering place, but the only people there were some guards along the edge of the city and several older couples who were maintaining the temple. Everyone else had gone to nearby camps. We stayed in Nauvoo for a few days before traveling back to Utah. We reached Wallsburg, and then we came here."

Nathan spoke up again. "Aren't you leaving out a key event that happened in Nauvoo?"

Marie smiled. "Oh, I almost forgot. Nathan and I were sealed in the Nauvoo Temple during that time. The Lord was truly watching out for us. Well, I think I'll turn the time over to my mother."

Carol took the microphone and said, "Yes, it was a big shock to find out these two got married during their little journey! That's okay. I guess the era of fancy wedding receptions is over anyway."

"Thank goodness!" a middle-aged man called out, motioning to his four teenage daughters sitting next to him. The group laughed, and a few other parents expressed their relief that things were returning to a simpler lifestyle.

Once they settled down, Carol continued, "I was in a unique position when the prophet's invitation came to gather. My husband Aaron has been working for the Church as a double agent, you could say. He works at the National Security Agency's facility near the Point of the Mountain, and he has witnessed firsthand that the government is doing horrible things behind the scenes. Aaron has been keeping the General Authorities up to date on what is happening, so he and I had to stay behind. Plus, we were watching over Denise."

"Then how come you came here?" a young girl asked.

"Well, things finally got so bad in Orem that I was in constant fear someone was going to break into our home. I just didn't feel safe anymore. So Denise and I tried to reach our ward's camp in Kamas. We were on our way there when the earthquake struck. We survived the shaking and ended up in the Wallsburg camp, where we were reunited with Nathan and Marie. But I just want to add my witness to Nathan's statement that you made the right choice to follow the prophet. I know it felt like a huge sacrifice at the time, but those who stayed in the valleys have paid a steep price many times over for doing so."

Carol then turned and handed the microphone to Denise, who hesitantly stood up.

"I don't have much to say, other than to share how grateful I am to be alive," Denise said. "My parents went to California after the big earthquake there, and they never came back. Carol's husband was able to track them with their chips, but we think my mom is dead, and we're not sure about my dad. Either way, I was lucky to have the Shaws take me in, and Carol has protected me."

She then pointed at Elder Cluff. "I do have a question for you, though. I'm not a member of the Church, but Nathan has been teaching me as we hiked along. He said I could become a member after we reached a camp. Well, we're here. Do you think we could baptize me before sundown?"

Denise's question brought smiles and chuckles from the group. Nathan stepped forward and said, "I truly believe she is ready. Elder Cluff, would it be possible for you to interview her?"

"I think that would be great," Elder Cluff said. "We haven't had a convert baptism since we got here! The lake might be very cold, though."

"I don't care," Denise said. "Let's do it!"

❧

Thirty minutes later the group had walked from the pavilion to the camp's lake. Denise's interview with Elder Cluff hadn't taken too long, and now she and Nathan stood at the water's edge, dressed in white clothing.

The autumn air was crisp as Nathan led Denise into the cold water, but Denise smiled at everyone and said, "It's just right."

Nathan felt a rush of emotion as he began the baptismal prayer, and his voice trembled as he said, "Denise Foster, having been commissioned of Jesus Christ, I baptize you in the name of the Father, and of the Son, and of the Holy Ghost. Amen."

Nathan submerged Denise in the water, and she had a wide grin as she surfaced. They gave each other a small embrace, then proceeded to the shore, where a folding chair was stationed. Elder Cluff joined Nathan, who quickly confirmed Denise a member of the Church of Jesus Christ of Latter-day Saints. They were both shivering, so Nathan kept the confirmation short. Once he concluded, they were escorted to a nearby cabin to change back into their regular clothes and warm up.

Elder Cluff called out, "Let's have everyone meet back at the pavilion to congratulate the newest member of the Church."

❧

Once they were back at the pavilion after Denise's confirmation, Nathan took Elder Cluff aside and said, "When I was in Nauvoo, the temple president showed me an e-mail that asked all maintenance missionaries to return to Salt Lake to help with the cleanup efforts. That was a while ago, though. Have you seen any updates about what I should do?"

"Not concerning your assignment, but we've received reports about situations in other areas of the state," Elder Cluff said. "It sounds like the earthquake left the Wasatch Front in shambles, and freeways such as I-80 through Parley's Canyon are very dangerous because gangs are attacking travelers. The Church is basically telling everyone to just stay put in the camps."

Nathan frowned. "I wish I could just stay here as well, but I feel an urgent need to get to Salt Lake. What do you suggest?"

"Well, it is your calling, so I feel you should follow Elder Miller's direction and make an effort to get there," Elder Cluff said. "You might be able to work your way around those criminals in Parley's Canyon, but I wouldn't risk it. So despite the destruction from the flood, I think your best chance is to make your way down Provo Canyon."

"That's what I was thinking," Nathan said.

"I wouldn't recommend going alone, though. Maybe one of our young men could go with you."

Marie was nearby, chatting with a friend she had known in high school. Nathan could hardly bear the thought of being separated from her again, but he didn't see any other options. He caught her attention and motioned for her to join them. She walked over and took his hand in hers.

"Elder Cluff agrees that I should try to reach Salt Lake," Nathan said. "You can stay here with your mom and Denise. We'll be together again soon."

Marie raised her eyebrows, then shook her head slowly. "When we got married, your mission became my mission too. I'm your companion now, and I'm going with you."

Nathan gave a quick glance at Elder Cluff, who merely shrugged and looked at the ground. Nathan stammered, "Um, I don't think the rule about being married has been clarified yet—"

"Exactly," Marie said. "You were going to ask Elder Miller about it when you saw him again. I might as well be standing right next to you when you do."

"That sounds good to me," Elder Cluff said with a grin.

Nathan rolled his eyes at his spunky wife, but inwardly he was thrilled. It would be dangerous for both of them, but it felt right.

"Okay,'" he told her. "Besides, we ought to check on your home in Orem and try to contact your dad."

CHAPTER 6

The U.N. convoy rolled north along I-15 through Utah without any opposition. In fact, they hardly saw anyone.

"Americans once lived in these towns, correct?" Commander Klopov asked Garrett as they took a brief break in the parking lot of an abandoned gas station on the outskirts of Beaver.

"I think they're still around, but I'll bet they've had advance notice we were coming and have cleared out of the way."

"I can't blame them," Klopov said. "It seems that many of the people on 'the list' are from Utah."

"What list is that?" Garrett asked.

"Haven't I told you about it before?" Klopov responded. "It's a list of 'troublemakers' that the U.S. government compiled. They are mostly religious fanatics or people who are suspected of fleeing to the mountains."

"That's very interesting," Garrett said. "Is the government actively searching for these people?"

"I think they are, but they're shifting the responsibility to us now," Klopov said. "I heard that near Salt Lake the government supposedly built concrete detention camps to keep the people in. I'm eager to see how those worked out. Maybe we can use them."

"I wonder if anyone I know is on the list," Garrett told him. "If so, I could help find them."

"Feel free to look it over while we rest," Klopov said. "I've got it saved on this computer. Let me pull it up for you."

He took a laptop from a compartment in the vehicle and punched a few keys. Then he handed it to Garrett.

"You can sort the list by name or location," Klopov said. "Let me know if you recognize anyone. Like you said, maybe we can pay them a visit."

"I'll see who I can find."

Garrett took the laptop to a nearby picnic table and typed in "Foster" and "Utah." There were more than 100 people listed, so he narrowed it down to Orem. A familiar name popped up.

Foster, Nathan

Garrett clicked on the name, and his son's photo appeared next to a column of information that read:

*** High-profile fugitive
Member of the LDS Church
LDS missionary for two years in Minnesota
Microchip implant: No
Current whereabouts unknown

A mix of emotions surged through him. According to the government, Nathan was still out there somewhere. That's all he could hope for.

Garrett closed the file and took the laptop back to Klopov, who asked, "Did you find who you were looking for?"

"Actually, I did. A son from my first marriage. He's a Mormon, so I'm not too shocked they put him on the list. They don't know where he is now, though. Neither do I."

"Your son is a Mormon?" Klopov asked in genuine surprise. "I would've disowned him."

Garrett merely nodded, but deep down his resentment toward the big Russian grew just a little bit more.

CHAPTER 7

"You know where to find us," Carol said, giving Marie a hug at the entrance of the Heber Valley Camp. "We'll stay here until we hear from you."

Elder Cluff had agreed to let them drive a four-wheeler down the canyon to Heber City, with Paul and Jake following behind on a second one. They reached the flood zone and realized the four-wheeler wouldn't be much use in navigating through the piles of mud, tree limbs and shattered houses. So they came to a stop and turned the vehicle over to Jake.

"Good luck," Paul said. "Things have dried up a bit, but it's still a mess."

"This is eerie," Marie said. "It was one thing to see massive destruction in the Midwest, but this is Heber!"

Nathan and Marie walked for a few miles toward Provo Canyon. The stench of decay and death was everywhere, and Marie gagged several times. She didn't complain, though, and Nathan appreciated her determination.

By that evening they reached the location where the east end of Deer Creek Reservoir had been. It was now just a wide expanse of mud. They spent a cold night huddled together, and by sunrise they were walking along the edge of the canyon on what was left of Highway 189.

Nathan studied the exposed lake bed, and he noticed the Provo River was running steadily along its original course through the bottom of the canyon.

"Hey, look for something we could float on," he told Marie. "It would make our trip go a lot faster."

Within a minute Marie pointed out a canoe that had been partially buried by the flood. They worked for twenty minutes to get it loose, and they were thrilled to see a paddle lodged under the center seat.

"I don't see any holes in it," Nathan said. "It should work."

They dragged it about fifty yards through ankle-deep mud to the river, then they carefully climbed in. Soon they were moving along at a good pace.

As they approached the location where the Deer Creek Dam had been, they paddled to the edge of the river and stepped out onto the bank. They expected to find a 100-foot drop-off, but to their surprise there wasn't much left of the dam. The river had carved a path through the remains of the dam, and there weren't many obstacles to deal with.

"Are you willing to give it a try?" Nathan asked.

Marie took another look down the canyon, then nodded. "I think we'll make it."

Once they got going again, Marie quickly wondered if they had made the right choice. They hit a stretch of concrete rubble, and they bounced along like they were in a pinball machine. Miraculously, the canoe didn't overturn or get punctured.

Within an hour they were paddling past where Vivian Park had been, but nothing was recognizable. Even the old train car that had stood near the park's entrance was nowhere to be seen, although a section of the Heber Creeper's tracks was still in place.

Nathan had expected to see a lot of vehicles or even bodies, but the power of the water from two reservoirs roaring though this narrow part of the canyon had scoured everything clean.

❧

They continued to make good time, and soon they discovered where everything had ended up. As they emerged from Provo Canyon, they saw the river disappeared into a towering pile of junk that spread from the north canyon wall all the way up onto the ridge leading into Orem. Every imaginable item was thrown together into a monstrous mess where the canyon had widened. The highway overpass across the river had created a barrier for all of the debris, and the junk had compacted together for several hundred yards.

"Look out!" Marie shouted. "We're going to crash!"

"We don't have a choice," Nathan responded as the canoe slammed into the remains of a house. The canoe started to tip, but Nathan grabbed onto a piece of wood jutting from the house and pulled the canoe sideways against it.

"Climb out," he told Marie, and she carefully stepped from the canoe onto the house. They made their way through the soggy dumping ground, accompanied by the sound of creaking wood and metal with water rushing beneath it. Thankfully, the debris had packed itself quite tightly, and it only took a few minutes for them to reach the plateau on the west side, heading into Orem.

"Whoa, look at that," Nathan said as they looked south into Utah Valley. The area known as The Riverbottoms was now just a mud pit. The walls of a few buildings still stood, but it looked like a hurricane had swept through the area.

"How could anyone have survived that?" Marie whispered.

≈

For the next hour they walked west along 800 North in Orem. They could see how the flood waters had come through the area at about 10 feet high, even up on the plateau, and then had lowered as the water spread out. Even so, every home and building had been soaked by a few feet of water, and the smell of mold and decay was almost overpowering. No one could be seen.

"Marie, do you even want to bother going to your house?" Nathan asked. "That whole neighborhood probably got hit pretty hard."

"I know, but I want to see the house one last time," she said.

"Even if my dad isn't there, maybe I can salvage a few things."

They reached State Street and walked south. Marie couldn't remember a time that the road hadn't been filled with cars. Now they walked down the middle of the road without worry, other than avoiding the flood debris that covered the road at most of the intersections where the water had rushed through. They started to see more people, and Marie began to feel nervous.

"I can see why Mom felt it was time to get out of Orem," she said. "We might need to do our 'Black Flu' trick again if someone approaches us."

They just walked purposefully forward, and the few people that started following them soon gave up the chase. However, sunset came sooner than they had anticipated. Nathan had a flashlight, but they were worried the light might draw unwanted attention in the darkness.

They safely passed the Orem City offices, but they were still several blocks away from Marie's home. Nathan pondered where they could hide, then he took Marie's hand and led her toward the Orem City Library.

A window was broken on the main floor, and they slipped inside. The earthquake had knocked most of the books off the shelves, so Nathan moved a few of the shelves to create a makeshift structure they could hide beneath. They found some couch cushions and an old blanket that would have to suffice as bedding.

"Thanks for sticking with me," Nathan said as Marie cuddled against him in the darkness. "It seems like we spend way too much time sleeping in abandoned museums, libraries . . ."

Marie laughed. "What's that old saying? 'Home is where the heart is.' I could have stayed at the camp, but I'm glad I came with you."

Nathan pulled her closer and said, "I'm glad you did too."

CHAPTER 8

Garrett Foster was anxious to see what had become of Utah Valley after the earthquake. He was riding in the U.N. convoy's lead vehicle next to Commander Klopov as they crested the hill on I-15 in Santaquin and began descending into southern Utah Valley.

"The NSA Data Center is at the other end of this valley," Garrett said. "On a normal day, we would be there within an hour, but I would suspect we'll encounter many obstacles caused by the earthquake, such as floodwater and cracked roadways."

"We'll go as far as we can," Klopov said, noting the approaching darkness. "Besides, we should wait until mid-morning to occupy the NSA site. We want all of the employees there so they can help operate the systems."

"That's a valid point," Garrett said.

As they continued northward, Klopov pointed out a building east of the freeway that Garrett hoped he wouldn't notice—the Payson Temple.

"What is that?" the Russian asked.

Garrett calmly looked over at the temple. "Oh, that's just a Mormon temple. You'll see a few of them as we pass through the valley, but they're all abandoned. Their people—including my son, I suppose—all fled into the mountains. There's no point in checking them out."

Klopov gave him a sideways glance. "If you say so."

In between Payson and Spanish Fork, they began to see the remnants of a massive flood. Mud and garbage covered the freeway.

The five-axled transporters had no trouble plowing forward through the muck, but as they reached Springville, there was still standing water on the freeway.

"This is deeper than I've ever seen," Garret said. "The dams up Provo Canyon must've burst to cause all of this flooding. I don't trust driving through this water much longer. If the freeway is broken up, we could drop into a hole and never get out. We ought to go into Springville and take our chances along the foothills."

Klopov agreed, and the U.N. convoy took Springville's southern exit. The flooding was evident all the way to the railroad tracks on the west side of town, but then things began to dry out. They turned north on Springville's Main Street and made good time crossing over Ironton Hill into Provo. The power was evidently out, and the moon was hidden from view by the mountains. It was hard to see anything beyond their headlights.

Garrett guided them up University Avenue and then cut across to State Street heading into Orem. A full moon was now visible, and they could see tremendous signs of flood damage, but they continued to just crunch through any debris in their way.

"How far are we from the NSA Center?" Klopov asked.

"Oh, probably less than twenty miles," Garrett said.

"Then let's find a good location we could park the convoy that isn't too far off the freeway. We'll cover the rest of the distance in the morning."

"Okay," Garrett said. "There's a university just on the other side of this ridge with some large parking lots. There will be plenty of room for our equipment."

"That should work," Klopov said.

Ten minutes later Garrett was leading the U.N. convoy into Utah Valley University's student parking lots. The vehicles formed their customary defensive formation as they pulled to a stop.

Garrett was filled with a mixture of relief and sadness to be so close to his home, which was only a mile away. Could Denise still be somewhere nearby?

❧

Garrett had a restless night's sleep. At 6 a.m. he finally went to Commander Klopov's sleeping compartment in the back of the transporter. He knew the commander was always up promptly at 5:45 each morning, so he knocked gently and waited.

Within a few seconds the door opened.

"What do you need?" Klopov growled. "I thought we weren't going to move out until eight o'clock."

"You're right," Garrett said. "I wanted to ask a favor, though. As you know, I'm from Utah. My home is a short distance from here. I would like to take a jeep and see if there is any chance my daughter is still alive."

Garrett knew there was a very slim chance that Klopov would let him go, but he had been a model soldier, and they still had two hours before their scheduled departure. Klopov started shaking his head, but then said, "Oh, get out of here. Be back in an hour."

❧

Twenty minutes later, Garrett parked the jeep in front of his house. The neighborhood was quiet, and it was clear that the flooding had been a few feet deep even there.

He walked up the front sidewalk and stood at the front door. He realized how surreal it was. A year ago he would have walked through the door and found his beautiful wife and daughter waiting to greet him. Now he didn't know what he'd find.

He entered the living room and immediately noticed that the house had been ransacked.

"Denise?" he called out. "Are you here?"

He hurried to her bedroom and saw that it was essentially bare. All of her possessions were gone, even little keepsakes and trinkets that thieves would have never taken.

"Where would she have gone?" he thought. They weren't

particularly close with anyone, and Nathan was off doing his Church service work. An idea popped into his head that maybe she had moved in with the Shaws.

He ran back to the jeep and made the quick drive to the Shaws' home. The door was ajar, and he walked right in. The flooding had been minimal, and their house hadn't been torn apart. He went to the kitchen and opened the fridge, releasing a small burst of putrid air. He noticed there were apples inside that looked fairly fresh. Someone had clearly been living there, maybe as recently as when the earthquake struck.

He moved into other areas of the house, and in a back bedroom he found what he was looking for—a framed photo of himself with Vanessa and Denise. There were other items in the room that Denise had cherished, and he was puzzled why she would have left them behind.

"Maybe things got too unsafe and they took off," he told himself.

Garrett picked up the framed photo and tucked it under his arm. He sensed Denise was still alive somewhere and wanted to stay longer to uncover additional clues, but he checked his watch. He only had a few minutes to get back to UVU within the hour he had promised Klopov. The last thing he needed was to get on the Russian's bad side.

CHAPTER 9

Nathan and Marie had awakened in the Orem City Library just after 6 a.m. and they both felt an urgency to get moving. They had walked along Center Street and marveled at the damage the flood had caused even this far from the mouth of Provo Canyon.

Throughout the city they could see small plumes of smoke, as if the remaining residents were cooking their breakfasts on campfires or just trying to stay warm. The few people they had seen the previous evening had purposely turned away from them or shouted at them to "get lost."

"Who would have thought 'survival of the fittest' would happen right here in Orem?" Marie asked as they watched an older woman scurry around a corner in fear after they spotted her.

They soon approached Marie's home, and as they turned the street corner, they were surprised to see a jeep parked in front of the house. Judging by the fresh tire tracks through the mud and debris in the road, it had just recently arrived. They crept closer and saw the jeep had a United Nations logo on the door.

"This can't be good," Marie whispered. "Maybe they're looking for my dad."

Nathan nodded and motioned for her to follow him. They moved quietly to a home across the street and hid behind an abandoned car in the driveway.

"All we can do is wait," Nathan said. "I don't dare do anything else."

They peered over the hood of the car, watching for any sign of who might be in Marie's home. They didn't have to wait long. The front door opened, and they saw a man in a U.N. uniform emerge. He looked across the street in their direction.

"Get down," Marie hissed, and they both ducked behind the car. The man slammed the front door, and he was close enough they could hear the clomping of his boots as he walked back to the jeep. Nathan popped up his head to take a look as the U.N. soldier pulled away, but all he could see was the back of the man's head.

Once the jeep had disappeared around the corner, Nathan said, "At least the guy didn't have your dad with him. Let's go take a look inside the house."

They cautiously crossed the street and entered the home. For the most part, everything looked in place, other than the slight residue from the flood water. Marie saw footprints leading to the fridge. She opened it to see the apples and other items.

"Someone has been living here," she said. "I'm sure it was Dad."

Nathan came to her side and peered in the fridge. His eyes instantly lit up, and he grabbed an apple.

"That U.N. guy must be eating pretty well," he said. "I can't believe he left this food alone."

They checked the rest of the house, and Marie noted how Denise had been staying in her bedroom. Carol had told her that when they chatted in Wallsburg, but now it really sunk in. Denise hadn't disturbed any of her possessions, and Marie gazed around the bedroom she hadn't been in since leaving for Chicago several months earlier.

"Wow, my life sure has changed," she said softly. She sat on the bed and sobbed, letting out months of pent-up emotions. Nathan had been checking other rooms in the house, and he rushed to her side when he heard her cries.

"What happened?" he asked. "Are you okay?"

She reached out to him, and he sat down beside her. She motioned toward a framed photo collage from her days at the University of Utah, and a poster she had bought at a Taylor Swift concert in 2015.

"These things mean nothing now," Marie said as she wiped her eyes. "These are tears of gratitude. I've got my priorities back in order, and I'm married to the greatest man in the world. I've been blessed."

✑

They searched the house for a few minutes more before deciding to grab any unspoiled food from the fridge and cupboards and stuff it into their backpacks. Then they went outside and started following the jeep's tire tracks, hoping to figure out what the U.N. soldier had been doing.

The jeep seemed to be backtracking on its own path, and soon they came to the crest of a hill overlooking the Utah Valley University campus. In the parking lots below they saw a large contingent of U.N. vehicles, including some strange huge machines with five axles.

"Whoa," Nathan said. "It looks like our U.N. soldier wasn't alone."

Several vehicles began to drive out of the parking lot, and they headed north on 1200 West. Nathan and Marie climbed into a nearby tree for a better view, and they watched for fifteen minutes as the convoy left the parking lot. In the distance they could see the lead vehicles had taken the Orem Center Street onramp and were now traveling on I-15 toward Salt Lake.

"What are they doing here?" Marie asked. "Do you think they're coming to help us clean up after the earthquake?"

"Maybe, but I think they have a bigger objective than that," Nathan said, pointing toward the northwest.

"What's over there?" Marie asked. "Thanksgiving Point?"

"No. The NSA Data Center."

CHAPTER 10

Garrett stared out the window of the U.N. transporter, stunned by the destruction before his eyes in northern Utah County. The effects of the flooding were still evident, but as the U.N. convoy journeyed up the broken remains of I-15, he gawked at what he saw. Homes and businesses looked like they had been tossed in the air and then slammed back down. Destruction was evident as far as he could see.

He searched the valley's western slopes and could faintly see the NSA Data Center in the distance.

"See those buildings on the hill over there?" Garrett asked Commander Klopov, who was seated next to him. "That's where we are going."

Klopov grunted. "They don't look too impressive. I expected to see skyscrapers."

"They actually go very deep into the ground because the government didn't want them to attract attention. I'm pretty sure they have their own electrical generating station as well. So the whole complex is much bigger than it looks."

"Whatever. It's the data that matters to me. If we get control of those computers, we'll control the nation."

They reached the 2100 North exit in Lehi, and from that point on the freeway looked impassible, even for their five-axle machines. Garrett stared at the Point of the Mountain. The hills of sand had spread out like a scoop of melted Jell-O, covering the buildings and roads below them.

"We better take this exit," Garrett said. "It will get us close.

Then we ought to get vehicles on every side of the NSA complex before we move in. Otherwise the employees might try to escape."

"I agree," Klopov said. He then got on the radio and made assignments for each vehicle.

Their plans were delayed as they reached the Jordan River. The river was still running high, but the peacekeepers gazed in amazement at the deep gorge that had been carved out. The spot had been a bottleneck for the floodwaters coming out of Utah Lake and heading downstream toward the Great Salt Lake.

"We have no choice but to dig out the banks and level out a path so we can get down there," Klopov said.

They had brought along heavy equipment from Las Vegas, and it had come in handy on several sections of the freeway, but this was the biggest project yet. After two hours and only minimal progress, Klopov became impatient.

"We need to get there," he said. "I'm sure the employees have seen us and are probably taking off. Get one of the inflatable rafts. We'll cross the river and walk there."

Klopov, Garrett, and 30 other men made their way down the river bank, and one of the soldiers swam across the river with a rope tied to his belt. When he reached the other side, he secured the rope tightly around a large rock, and then the two leaders crossed in the raft, pulling themselves along with the rope. They then made their way up the hillside as the remaining soldiers were ferried across the river. Once everyone was across, they walked west until they reached Redwood Road, then headed toward the NSA buildings.

They moved briskly along, pausing briefly to look at a car that had nose-dived into a crevice in the road. Blood splatters were still evident, although the driver's body had been removed.

"This must've been quite an earthquake," Klopov said. "The driver hardly had time to stop."

They finally approached the gate to the NSA Data Center and expected a confrontation, but there weren't any guards on duty.

They walked to the closest building and knocked loudly. A large bearded man cautiously opened the door. He stopped with a jolt, clearly surprised to see them.

"Are you from the United Nations?" he asked nervously.

"Yes," Klopov said. "Are you alone here?"

"No. Several staff members have stayed, although most have left to check on their families. We haven't received any directions for several days, so those of us who have stayed just kept monitoring the citizens. It's getting pretty bad across the country."

"Let's gather the remaining workers together," Klopov said. "I'd like to let them know they're going to be all right."

Ten minutes later Klopov stood before fifty workers who had come to the main conference room. Some seemed calm, but others were clearly bothered to have U.N. officers in the building.

"Do you have authorization from the U.S. government to be here?" a dark-haired man asked.

Klopov gave a small grin. "We were invited by your leaders to assist in the rebuilding of your country. They didn't specifically tell us to come here, but it will be beneficial for everyone in the long run if we have access to the information."

"I don't think so," the man said. He looked at the bearded man they had first met. "Gerald, this isn't right."

"Henry, stay calm," Gerald said, moving to stand between the employees and the soldiers. "We need to cooperate with them."

"He's right," Klopov said. "If you cooperate with us, you will live comfortably. Otherwise, you will be taken to a new location."

"Doesn't that make me a prisoner either way?" Henry asked defiantly. "I'd rather be dead."

Klopov didn't hesitate in giving a hand signal to one of the U.N. soldiers on his right. The soldier immediately lifted his rifle and shot Henry in the forehead. He dropped to the ground with a cry of pain, but was soon motionless in a pool of blood as the other NSA employees gasped and shrieked in fear. Some even dropped to their knees and averted their eyes from Klopov's gaze.

Klopov didn't even give Henry's body a second look. "If you choose to cooperate with us, form a line to my left. If not, stay where you are."

The message was clear. The remaining employees began shuffling to the left side of the room.

Garrett had watched the whole scene in semi-shock. He was surprised time and again by Klopov's ruthless techniques. His mind returned to the shooting of innocent citizens at the CasaBlanca casino in Mesquite. He felt sickened that his fellow "peacekeepers" continually resorted to violence to keep the people under control.

During the next hour, Klopov essentially reorganized the NSA employees and explained that their role was now boiled down to finding American citizens via their implanted microchips.

"We don't care about their e-mails or what they post on Facebook anymore," Klopov told the group. "We want you to use these tremendous computers to pinpoint people's locations. We'll take care of the rest."

Klopov then motioned for Garrett to follow him outside, where the transporters had finally made their way across the Jordan River and into the parking lot.

They walked toward the main communications vehicle and ordered the officer inside to contact his superiors. Within a few moments he was speaking via satellite to a leader inside the Kremlin in Russia.

"We have secured the NSA Data Center in Salt Lake City," Klopov said. "The U.S. government's data is now under our control. I'm confident the Coalition invasion can begin without interference."

Garrett felt weak in the knees and leaned against the transporter as Klopov continued his conversation. He knew that America had barely endured the troubles that had already happened. The citizens weren't prepared for what was coming next.

CHAPTER 11

Within only a couple of days, Carol and Denise became vital members of their new ward at the Heber Valley Camp. Since neither one had small children to care for, they were able to assist the Relief Society presidency in many ways. They also pitched in as the ward prepared for winter by collecting wood and securing the tents.

One afternoon Carol went into the forest to collect fallen limbs when she saw a woman dressed in white standing several yards up the hill. She stepped back in surprise as the woman glided down the slope toward her and said, "Carol, don't be afraid. It's me, Helen Foster."

Carol shook her head, amazed that Nathan's deceased mother now stood before her.

"Helen, you look so . . . good!"

Helen smiled. "Yes, the last time you saw me I was a bit shriveled up because of the cancer."

"This is fantastic," Carol said as she gazed at Helen's radiant features. "I guess we're in-laws now."

"We are," Helen said. "I was allowed to attend Nathan and Marie's sealing in the Nauvoo Temple, and it was marvelous. I wish you could have been there."

"Me too. They are a special couple," Carol said. "Thank you for appearing to me and letting me know that."

"Actually, there is more that I must tell you," Helen said. "I'm here on a special assignment. I have a dear friend in Spirit Prison who wants to enter Paradise. She wants to assist her family on earth.

We need you to perform the temple ordinances in her behalf."

"That should be possible," Carol said. "Yesterday they showed me the camp's tent temple. Who is your friend? Do I know her?"

"Vanessa Foster."

Carol was momentarily speechless, and Helen merely smiled as Carol digested that information.

Carol finally spoke. "So you're saying that you've become good friends with the woman who destroyed your marriage and ruined your life?"

"Yes. I have forgiven her. She never truly understood the ripple effect of her affair with Garrett until she experienced her life review after her death. But she has done everything she can to repent of her sins, and she is ready to move forward."

Carol shook her head. "Wow, I really admire you."

"When all is said and done, she is my sister in the gospel," Helen said. "The Savior's Atonement makes it possible to heal all wounds."

Helen then pointed up the hillside to where Carol had first seen her. "Look."

Carol saw a bright pinpoint of light appear that expanded until it was about 15 feet across. Inside it she could see Vanessa, as well as seemingly dozens of other people who were reaching out toward her. Although she couldn't hear their voices, she realized they were pleading with her to do their temple work.

"Vanessa has many relatives and ancestors who have been taught the gospel in the Spirit World and are eager to have their temple work done as well," Helen said. "Will you do it?"

"Of course," Carol said.

"Wonderful," Helen said. "Please go talk to Elder Cluff. He'll know what to do."

Helen then vanished, and the gap in the veil where Vanessa had stood also closed up. Carol found herself alone in the forest. She pinched herself and whispered, "Did that really happen?""

Her heart still was pounding, though, and she knew Helen had truly appeared to her. So she hurried back to the camp and found

Elder Cluff in one of the cabins.

"Can I talk to you privately for a minute?" she asked him.

"Sure." He motioned toward a small room at the back of the cabin. She stepped inside and he shut the door.

"You're probably going to think I'm crazy, but I just had a visit in the woods from one of my deceased neighbors, Helen Foster. She wants some temple work done for several people."

Elder Cluff shrugged slightly. "I don't think you're crazy. It has been happening here a few times a week. We have a room set up in the tent temple to record the information."

Carol felt relieved. "Thank you. Helen said you would know what to do."

"Let's go to the temple," Elder Cluff said. "It's a marvelous experience to participate in. I wish we could just transfer their Spirit World records straight into our laptops, but we can't. Helen will show you their records, and you'll have to type the information into the computer, but it sure beats the old way of not knowing who has accepted the gospel on the other side!"

❧

Elder Cluff and Carol made their way to the temple, and she marveled at the size of it, since it was made entirely of canvas.

"It's pretty amazing, isn't it?" he said. "There was some divine intervention in even getting it set up. We couldn't have done it alone."

They greeted a man standing at the temple entrance, who shook Elder Cluff's hand.

"We've had another request from beyond the veil," Elder Cluff said to the man. "So Carol is going to be in the Records Room for a while."

"Wonderful," the man said. "We love having names to do."

Elder Cluff first led her to a small room where a lady helped her select a white dress to wear.

"Thank you," Carol told the woman. "I'm nervous enough as it is, but this will help me feel the Spirit better. Helen was dressed in white, so I might as well be too."

After she had changed clothing, she met Elder Cluff again in the corridor. He led her to a small room toward the back of the temple, which contained a table and a chair. On the table was a large laptop computer and a laser printer. Carol could see a few sheets of blue and pink ordinance cards stacked beside the printer.

"This is our Records Room," he said. "It's a bit secluded from the rest of the temple, so you should have some privacy."

Carol motioned toward the stack of cards. "Are there a lot of ordinances being done?" she asked.

"Mainly for the living," Elder Cluff said. "There's actually been quite a bit of old-fashioned courting going on here at the camp. We hold dances regularly, and it seems to have sparked some romances. We seem to have a new engagement announced almost every day. As couples get together, we encourage them not to wait very long to get married. So the temple workers have been busy performing the temple ordinances and sealings for these camp members."

"That's how it should be," Carol said. "I know it really worked well for Marie and Nathan."

Elder Cluff smiled. "You're right, and these marriages are wonderful. The only problem we face right now is we don't have access to the Church's family history websites, so the work for the deceased has really slowed down. But as I said, we'll have more and more experiences like you had. I think they are getting impatient in the Spirit World, and so miracles are happening."

Elder Cluff sat down at the computer and logged in, then he motioned for Carol to sit down in front of it. He explained a few of the program's features and how to enter in the data, then he patted her on the back.

"I'll leave you alone now," he said. "Begin with a prayer, and everything else should take care of itself."

"Thank you," Carol said, suddenly feeling a bit apprehensive. "Please tell Denise where I am."

"I will. Take as long as you need, and enjoy the experience."

Once Elder Cluff had departed, Carol bowed her head and prayed. "Heavenly Father, thank thee for the privilege to assist in thy work. I ask thee to allow Helen to return once again, so that we might be able to help Vanessa progress in the Spirit World."

As she said those words, a white beam of light shone down through the temple's canvas roof. Carol watched in wonder as Helen materialized instantly in front of her within the light.

"Hello again," Helen said pleasantly. "Thank you for acting so promptly."

She was holding a large book with a silver cover, and she opened it to show Carol the first page. It contained a standard five-generation pedigree chart, with Vanessa's name on the first line.

"Are you going to get tired holding the book?" Carol said. "You could just place it on the table if you want."

Helen got an amused look, and then moved the book toward the corner of the table, but the book passed right through it.

"Now you see why I need to hold the book and turn the pages," she said. "Don't worry, I'm not going to get tired."

Carol laughed at herself. "Sorry. This is going to take some time to get used to—yet it feels so natural."

Helen held the book near the side of the computer screen, and Carol started typing in the information.

"Aaron had figured out through his job with the NSA that Vanessa had died, and it was somewhat of a relief for Denise to know that," Carol said. "But what about Garrett? Aaron said there was some sort of glitch showing he's still alive. Is that possible?"

Helen looked briefly troubled. "All I can say is he has not yet passed through the veil."

Carol raised her eyebrows. "So he isn't dead? Where is he?"

"I am not permitted to say more about him."

Carol nodded, knowing she had overstepped some sort of eternal boundary. "I apologize. I'll focus on our task at hand."

She then made rapid progress on entering the information for three dozen individuals. About twenty minutes later, they were finished.

"Your efforts will be a great blessing to this family," Helen said as she closed the silver book. "Thank you for your faithfulness. Be sure to let Nathan and Marie know how much I love them both."

Then as quickly as she arrived, Helen was gone.

Carol made sure to save the data, and then an overwhelming weariness encompassed her. She cried out for Elder Cluff as she slid out of the chair and onto the floor.

Within a few seconds, Elder Cluff and the woman who had helped her find a white dress entered the room.

"I feel almost paralyzed," Carol said. "What is wrong with me?"

Elder Cluff smiled. "Nothing is wrong. Our mortal bodies just aren't designed to handle that much glory for so long. We have another room where you can rest and get your strength back."

They guided her to a room with a nice bed and comfortable blankets. She sat on the edge of the bed and then lay down. They pulled a blanket over her, and she quickly drifted off to sleep, completely sapped, but with a huge grin on her face.

CHAPTER 12

Before departing, Elder Smith and Aaron had arranged for Elder Bushman and the guards to be in charge of the temple. Then they had spent the last two days hiking over the ridge from Salt Lake into Bountiful. The earthquake had caused several fissures and landslides across what had been a well-worn trail. The elderly apostle struggled with almost every step, but Aaron admired how he never complained about the situation.

"I think we're halfway there," Elder Smith would say during the steepest parts. "The temple should be in sight soon."

Late in the afternoon they reached the top of a ridge, and their eyes finally rested on the Bountiful Temple.

"See, I told you we were nearly there," Elder Smith said with a grin.

"It's a beautiful sight," Aaron responded. "We should be able to get there by sunset."

They climbed down the ridge and entered one of the highest subdivisions on the hill. The earthquake had made a mess of the roads and sidewalks, but maneuvering through the broken concrete and asphalt was still better than hiking the damaged trail.

When they were within a few blocks of the temple, they heard a whirring sound. They stopped and looked at the sky. Suddenly a black helicopter came over the ridge they had just been on. Aaron was partly in the road, while Elder Smith was standing near some bushes.

"Hide!" Aaron hissed to Elder Smith. "I'll take care of things."

Aaron stood motionless as the helicopter lowered to the ground.

A U.S. soldier jumped out with a semi-automatic rifle aimed at Aaron's chest.

"Come with me," he shouted.

Aaron slowly walked to the helicopter with his hands held high. The soldier moved behind him and put the barrel of the gun in his back, and another soldier jumped out and checked him for weapons. Once they were sure he was unarmed, they motioned for him to climb into the helicopter.

Aaron peered inside and saw he wasn't the only prisoner. There were eight other men staring back at him. They looked terrified. From his work at the NSA, he knew the government was rounding people up like cattle in big cities where there had been riots or natural destruction. He never dreamed he would become one of them.

The soldiers closed the door and the helicopter lifted off again.

"As we approached you, I tried to detect your chip, but we couldn't get a reading," the first soldier said. "That's why we detained you. Do you have an explanation?"

Aaron looked into the man's eyes. "Please spare my life, sir," Aaron said contritely. "I'm willing to cooperate with you. I worked at the NSA Center. I have valuable information."

"Then why don't you have a chip?" the solider asked.

"I cut it out myself," Aaron replied, holding up his hand so they could better see the jagged scar where the chip once was.

The soldiers looked at each other in surprise.

"This guy is crazy," the second soldier said. "Let me shoot him, and we can toss him out the side door."

"Calm down," the first one said. "Shooting him now would just make a mess. If he's telling the truth, maybe we'll get some brownie points from the commander for bringing him in."

Aaron bowed his head, grateful to be spared. Then the first soldier kicked him in the ribs, making Aaron gasp in pain. The soldiers laughed before moving to the front of the helicopter.

A captured man near Aaron whispered, "This sure doesn't feel like America anymore, does it?"

Aaron shook his head. "Everything has been turned upside down. Satan must be celebrating."

❧

Elder Smith emerged from the bushes and watched the helicopter fly in a southwest direction toward the Salt Lake Valley. Everything had happened so fast. One moment he and Aaron were peacefully walking along, and the next moment Aaron was a prisoner.

"Heavenly Father, please protect Aaron, and give me strength to make it to safety, if it be thy will."

The apostle felt a surge of renewed energy, and he hurried toward the temple. Within minutes, he reached the outer fence. A guard came toward him. "Elder Smith? Is that you?"

"Yes. Please help me inside. I need to rest."

The guard took the apostle's arm and led him to the temple as another guard closed the gate behind them. Soon Elder Smith was in the temple president's office sharing his story. "Is my wife here?" he asked.

"We haven't seen her," the president said.

Elder Smith frowned. "She must still be somewhere here on the hillside. We need to find her."

CHAPTER 13

About forty miles away, Nathan and Marie stood atop what remained of the Point of the Mountain. They watched a black helicopter cross the valley and land at the base of the Bingham Copper Mine.

"This whole area is in shambles, but the government has enough resources to fly these helicopters around," Nathan said, shaking his head. "What a joke."

Nathan's thoughts drifted to the long, grueling walk from Orem they had endured. They had stayed far behind the slow-moving U.N. convoy as it traveled north on I-15. They didn't dare get near it and risk being spotted.

The convoy had reached the city of Lindon, where the freeway dropped in elevation. The vehicles had no choice but to stop, due to the flood debris strewn across all lanes of I-15.

Nathan and Marie had watched several U.N. officials get out of their vehicles and argue about what to do, but finally the big five-axle vehicles just started moving forward, crawling over the broken limbs and other garbage at about five miles an hour.

Nathan and Marie had briefly discussed going to the Mount Timpanogos Temple to see if anyone there could help them, but it was so prominent on the hillside that they were afraid the U.N. convoy might go check it out.

It was somewhat of a relief when the vehicles had reached Lehi and turned off I-15 toward the NSA Data Center. That allowed Nathan and Marie to pick up their pace and reach the Point of the Mountain before sunset.

Nathan now looked to the north and sighed. The Salt Lake Valley looked even worse than Utah Valley. There was a huge gaping sinkhole in the south end of the valley that reached from Sandy on the east all the way into Bluffdale.

"That hole must be at least five miles across," he said. "I can't even imagine how many people died there."

Marie sat on the ground, feeling physically and emotionally exhausted. The sights that surrounded her were overwhelming.

"I need to sleep," she said. "We can keep going in the morning."

Nathan knew she was right, but couldn't imagine sleeping out in the open.

"I know you're tired, but we should keep moving," he said. "We need to find shelter before dark."

"Okay," she said. "My legs feel like rubber, though. Let's pray about what to do."

Nathan agreed, and he said a prayer asking for guidance. As he raised his head and opened his eyes, the sun glinted off something along the foothills to the east. Nathan squinted and saw the glint of the Angel Moroni on the spire on the Draper Temple. He hadn't even thought about that temple until that moment, but the earthquake had shifted the hill enough that the edifice was now visible.

"Now that was a miracle," he said, pointing to the temple. "Your prayers have been answered."

≈

It took another two hours for them to reach the Draper Temple. The sun had slipped behind the mountains as they reached the gate, but once Nathan had given the password to a guard, they were quickly ushered inside the perimeter fence and allowed into the temple.

The temple was being guarded by six high priests. The main guard introduced himself as Brother Witten. He explained that their wives had recently been led to a mountain camp due to the violence that had erupted in the area after the earthquake.

"Have people been trying to get inside the fence?" Marie asked.

"Yes," Brother Witten said. "Just last week we had to use the power of the priesthood to repel a large group who demanded we give them food. They had some guns and started shooting at the temple."

"What did you do?" Nathan asked.

"We simply called upon the powers of heaven to intervene," the man said. "Within seconds, they all started scurrying down the hill. We don't know what they saw, but it scared them enough that they haven't been back."

"Well, I really need to get in touch with Elder Wilford Miller at the Bishop's Storehouse," Nathan said. "He's my supervisor, and he wanted me to meet with him, but I don't think I can get across the valley right now."

"It would be a challenge," Brother Witten said. "But don't worry, we should be able to contact Elder Miller through the ZOOM network."

"That would be great," Nathan said.

One of the other men brought a laptop into the room, and within a couple of minutes Brother Witten was speaking to Elder Miller in a video chat.

"I've got one of your maintenance missionaries here in the Draper Temple," Brother Witten told him. "I'll let him speak to you."

Brother Witten handed the laptop to Nathan, and Elder Miller's face lit up.

"Elder Nathan Foster! I wasn't sure I'd ever see you again!"

Nathan chuckled. "I felt the same way a few times. But I'm doing well. I followed the Spirit and helped a good friend escape from Chicago. Then we've been working our way back to Utah."

"That's great, because I need you to take on an important assignment. You might want to take your friend along as well."

Nathan shifted the laptop so Elder Miller could see Marie, who was sitting next to him. "I'm glad to hear that, because my good friend is now my wife."

The look on Elder Miller's face was priceless, but he kept his composure as Nathan and Marie smiled back at him.

"Wife?" he asked. "Please explain how that happened."

Nathan then told him about their journey to the Nauvoo Temple and how they were sealed there by President Golding.

"That is wonderful," Elder Miller said. "The Spirit is confirming to me that it is the Lord's will—not that I can do much about it!"

They all laughed, and then Elder Miller grew more serious.

"I actually had you coming back to Salt Lake for a different reason. Now that the earthquake has closed off the canyons, we are asking the smaller 'white' camps that have been in place since spring to take everything they can and travel to larger gathering areas."

"So we are going to abandon those camps?" Nathan asked.

"Yes. The smaller camps served their purpose and worked well during the summer, but as we head into winter it'll be safer for the Saints to gather to larger camps, such as near the Manti and Logan temples. I have all of the maintenance missionaries helping with this change and taking additional supplies to the camps before things get worse."

"Where would you like us to go?" Nathan asked.

"Well, another urgent situation has come up," he said. "You must get to the Bountiful Temple as soon as possible. It won't be easy, but stick to the foothills."

Marie looked like she was going to cry. "Elder Miller, I'm so worn out. I don't know if I can make it. Could I stay here for a while?"

Elder Miller looked thoughtful. "No, the Spirit says otherwise. I feel you need to stay with Nathan. Let me talk to Brother Witten."

Nathan handed the laptop to the guard, and Elder Miller told him, "I authorize you to let Nathan take one of your four-wheelers to make the journey."

"Sounds good," Brother Witten said. "We'll make sure they are fully stocked up on food and gas for the trip."

He handed the laptop back to Nathan, who asked Elder Miller, "What are we needed there for?"

"When you get there, you'll find out," he said. "I wish I could tell you more. I'll be praying for you."

CHAPTER 14

Garrett slammed the door on his U.N. transporter and surveyed his surroundings. He was in the small town of Copperton, situated at the base of the Kennecott Copper Mine on the west side of the Salt Lake Valley. The town's higher elevation had kept it free from the flood waters, and the earthquake's destruction had been less severe there. The plan was for Copperton to be the U.N. headquarters in the valley until the floodwater subsided in downtown Salt Lake.

Commander Klopov had left a portion of the U.N. convoy at the NSA Center to keep things operating smoothly, then he and Garrett had traveled with the remaining peacekeepers to Copperton.

Their task was to sort through and organize the remaining U.S. citizens that had been detained. For Garrett, the whole process was a bit surreal. In California, he had been captured and interrogated by U.N. officers, and now he would be on the other side of the table deciding the fate of his fellow citizens.

During the era of martial law, the U.S. Army had established "detention centers" for citizens who were considered "troublemakers." They had built a series of camps near Tooele and in the Cedar Valley. These camps were more like outdoor holding pens with only one entrance. They had 12-foot-high concrete walls with razor sharp barbwire on the top. There were no barracks, toilet facilities, or shelter provided of any kind. There was no privacy at all.

Once these structures were built, the government began rounding people up who didn't fully cooperate or couldn't pay their debts. People were just thrown in these enclosures without so much as a bottle of water. Deaths occurred daily in these camps.

After the earthquake, though, it was more difficult to maintain these various enclosures, so a main concentration camp was established at the Kennecott Copper Mine. The mine was a massive pit hundreds of feet deep that served as a natural prison. It could hold thousands of prisoners without any real effort. The prisoners were just transported to the bottom of the pit with no shelter and basically left to fend for themselves.

Twice a day the guards would use a catapult to launch a few boxes of water and food supplies into the pit. They really didn't care whether the prisoners starved to death or not, but it was really entertaining to watch them fight like dogs over the food and water. The guards would pull out their binoculars and have a grand time watching the battles.

A few of the prisoners were clearly stronger and more malicious than the others, and they typically collected the most food each day. In contrast, many prisoners feared for their lives and didn't want to take part in the violence. They would usually go find a spot away from everyone else and slowly waste away.

Enough captives were dying that every couple of days the guards would drive a dump truck into the pit and force a few unlucky prisoners to gather up the bodies and put them in the truck bed. Then the dump truck would empty its load in a certain spot that was nicknamed "Mormon Hill." The guards would force the prisoners at gunpoint to cover the bodies with dirt by hand. It was a horrible task, and many prisoners secretly wished they could trade places with the deceased.

꙰

Three days had passed since Garrett began evaluating the prisoners, and he was already tired of it. Now that the U.N. was handling the decision-making, the U.S. Army soldiers were emptying the concentration camps around the area and bringing the captives to Copperton. Many of the prisoners they brought were gaunt and weak. The whole process made Garrett sick to his stomach.

Unfortunately, very few of the prisoners had skills that the Coalition needed. The new society needed blue-collar workers, such as farmers and plumbers, to get everything running again, but such citizens seemed to be in short supply. Instead, Garrett and his fellow U.N. officers saw a steady stream of bankers, lawyers, computer technicians, and administrative assistants. Many of them were still wearing the same clothes they had on when the earthquake hit.

The U.N.'s sorting procedure was the same as it had been in Long Beach. There were two options. A person who didn't fit the Coalition's needs was taken to the left and put on a bus, which would take them straight to the copper mine's pit of death.

If someone was considered suitable, they were taken to the nearby Copperton City Park and put inside what had been the city tennis courts. It now functioned well as a large wire cage within sight of the line of prisoners that Garrett was evaluating. It seemed like a worse fate to be put in the cage than to get on the bus, but only the U.N. officers knew the truth.

❧

The day dragged on, and Garrett's patience was growing thin as one lady proudly spouted off about the upper-level class on human behavior she had taught at the local community college.

Garrett held up his hand. "Ma'am, are you a Mormon?"

"I am."

"Then why are you here?" Garrett asked.

"What do you mean?"

"Didn't your prophet tell you to go to the mountains a few months ago?"

"Uh, well, I had my job at the college that I couldn't give up, plus I didn't want to lose my 401k . . ."

"How did that work out for you?" he asked.

She shrugged. "Not bad, I guess, until now."

Garrett tilted his head and gave her a half-grin. "It seems to me the proper human behavior would have been to follow your religious leader."

"Maybe, but I didn't want to go hide somewhere," she said. "I wanted to still make a difference in the world."

"So you think you can contribute to our new society?" Garrett asked.

"Absolutely," she said, staring into his eyes.

Garrett nodded slowly. "Okay, you've convinced me. Please go take a seat on the bus."

"Thank you," she gushed. "You won't regret it."

As she hurried off to the bus, Garrett's partner nudged him with his elbow and said, "Well done."

CHAPTER 15

Two days later, Nathan and Marie stood on a ridge looking down at the Bountiful Temple. They had endured a treacherous time on the four-wheeler trying to reach the temple. Many of the roads were still blocked and hadn't been repaired at all.

They had seen many people still wandering around the neighborhoods or sitting on porches. People would yell, "Hey, are you with the government? When are you gonna come help us?"

On two occasions, Nathan heard gunshots and wondered if he was the intended target. He often had to make some tough maneuvers to keep the four-wheeler from falling into a few crevices caused by the earthquake, but he always seemed to find a narrow way through, with Marie holding on tightly behind him.

The farther north they traveled along the Salt Lake foothills, the fewer people they saw. They had emptied the gas tank by the time they reached the University of Utah, but thankfully the guards at the Draper Temple had provided a five-gallon can that had been strapped to the back.

While Nathan refilled the tank, Marie looked across the valley. "Is that water?" she had asked, pointing down past the Church Office Building.

Nathan looked where she was pointing, and indeed there was a smooth sheet of water stretching from the downtown area all the way to the Great Salt Lake.

"I'm afraid so," he said, shaking his head. "We won't be going that way. We'll have to find another route."

The flooded valley forced them to do some steep off-road riding over the ridge to Bountiful, leading them to where they now stood. Darkness was coming quickly.

"As much as I'd like to get to the temple tonight, it's farther than it looks," Nathan said. ""Let's find a place to sleep."

❧

After spending the night huddled together above Bountiful underneath a scrub oak bush, Nathan and Marie started out on the four-wheeler once again. As they reached the upper streets of Bountiful, Marie felt a powerful impression.

"Have Nathan stop. Then listen."

Marie tapped Nathan on the shoulder and said in his ear, "Turn off the engine."

He gave her a sideways glance, but he did as she requested. They came to a stop, and he asked, "What do you need?"

She climbed off the back of the four-wheeler and walked to the edge of the road. "Shh," she said. "Listen."

They waited in silence for a few moments. Marie could only hear the chirping of a few birds, but then faintly came a voice from a wooded area below them.

"Hello! Can you hear me?" a woman cried. "Help me!"

Nathan and Marie looked at each other. "You can hear that, right?" she asked.

"I do," he said. He locked the brake on the four-wheeler, and they started walking toward the voice down in a cluster of trees.

"We hear you," Marie called out. "Keep talking. We're coming to help you."

Within a couple of minutes they spotted the roof of a wooden picnic shelter. The voice seemed to be coming from underneath it. Nathan hurried forward and tried to lift it, but it wouldn't budge. Then Marie joined him and with their combined effort they raised it a few inches, and an elderly woman wiggled out from under it.

Nathan and Marie dropped the shelter to the ground, and bent over the woman.

"Are you okay?" Marie asked.

"My arm is banged up, but I'll live," she said. "I had pretty much given up on being found until I heard your engine. How did you hear me over the noise?"

Marie shrugged. "A voice told me to stop."

"I'm glad you listened," the woman said.

"How did you get trapped?" Nathan asked. "Did this happen during the earthquake?"

"Yes, I am the visiting teacher to a single mom, and I would come watch her kids some mornings to give her a break. That's where I was headed when the earthquake hit. The sidewalk cracked and buckled in front of me, so I ran to this shelter, but one strong jolt sent it collapsing down on me! Thankfully I had my water bottle with me, or I might have died of thirst."

"We've got some water you can drink up at the four-wheeler," Nathan said. "No one else has come by?"

"I heard a lot of commotion up on the street. I yelled a lot, but I guess no one could hear me."

"May I look at your arm?" Marie asked. The woman nodded, and she winced as Marie gently touched her shoulder.

"Well, I don't think it's broken, but you need medical attention," Marie said. "We're going to the Bountiful Temple. Let us take you there."

"I would like that very much," the woman said. "I need to contact my husband. He's probably worried sick."

"Let me carry you," Nathan said. He picked her up, and Marie cleared the way ahead of them as they worked their way back to the four-wheeler. Nathan carefully placed her on the seat and said, "By the way, I'm Nathan Foster, and this is my wife Marie."

The woman stared at him as if she had seen a ghost. "Nathan Foster? This is unbelievable."

Nathan and Marie glanced at each other, slightly amused, as the woman continued, "You know my husband quite well— Elder Smith of the Quorum of the Twelve. You saved his life in Minnesota."

Nathan smiled in surprise. "Sister Smith? Wow. It's a pleasure to meet you!"

Sister Smith gave a small laugh. "We really owe you a lot, Nathan. That's twice you've saved us now."

❧

An hour later they arrived at the Bountiful Temple. Nathan had driven the four-wheeler slowly with Sister Smith positioned sideways behind him. Marie walked alongside to steady her.

They soon arrived at the front gate. Nathan gave the password to the guard stationed there, but he hardly acknowledged Nathan when he saw who the passenger was.

"Sister Smith!" the guard exclaimed. "We've looked all over for you! Elder Smith has been very worried."

"I'm glad to know he has missed me," she said with a grin. "Nathan, let's keep going."

They proceeded through the gate toward the temple as the guard got on his radio and notified the other temple guards what was happening.

As they reached the main temple doors, several people came out, including Elder Smith. He rushed to his wife's side and tenderly embraced her.

"It's a miracle," he said, looking into her eyes. "I was sure you had died."

"I was getting pretty close, but our family's guardian angel saved the day."

She motioned toward Nathan, and Elder Smith did a double-take as he saw his wife's rescuer. The two men briefly embraced, then Nathan said, "My wife Marie deserves the credit this time. The Spirit told her to have us stop, or else we would have ridden right past Sister Smith."

Elder Smith turned to Marie. "Thank you so much. This is a wonderful turn of events."

"Well, it isn't purely an accident we are in Bountiful," Nathan said. "Elder Miller of the Seventy told us to come here. Do you know why?"

"I do," Elder Smith said. "I must say I'm absolutely thrilled you're the one who got the assignment. I need to rejoin the remaining members of the Quorum of the Twelve. We are gathering in Rexburg."

Nathan raised his eyebrows and glanced at Marie as he thought about how hard it had been just to get from Salt Lake to Bountiful.

"We can do it," Marie said. "The Lord will help us."

Elder Smith smiled at her. "Thank you for your faith. We need to let Sister Smith recuperate a few days, but then we'll be on our way."

"Will the First Presidency be there too?" Nathan asked.

"Soon enough," Elder Smith said. "The prophet has some other matters of business to attend to, then he'll meet us in Idaho."

CHAPTER 16

A week later, Carol and Denise were helping wash the breakfast dishes at the Heber Valley Camp when they heard the news.

"There's going to be a Church broadcast this morning," one of the camp's priesthood leaders said. "Gather at the pavilion at 10 a.m. to watch it."

"Maybe we'll finally hear from the General Authorities," Carol said. "I'm eager to know what is going on."

The first weekend of October had come and gone without a General Conference, which was understandable with all of the destruction in Salt Lake. But since that time there had been much speculation in the camp about what was happening in the rest of the world, and with the Church in particular.

Several rows of folding chairs had been set up in the pavilion facing a large screen, and Carol and Denise found seats near the front. At 10 a.m., the screen flickered to life and a panoramic view of the south side of the Manti Temple was shown. Hundreds of people could be seen gathered on the lawn where the Mormon Miracle Pageant had been held each year. Large speakers that had been used as part of the pageant were positioned around the temple grounds.

"Where is that?" Denise whispered.

"It's the Manti Temple," Carol said. "It's in a small town about a hundred miles south from here."

The camera then zoomed in on a pulpit at the base of the temple. Two men in dark suits emerged and stood near the pulpit. One of the men leaned over to the microphone and said, "Please stand. We are privileged to have with us today our beloved prophet."

A unified gasp rose from the crowd, and everyone stood as a man came out of the temple and walked toward the pulpit. Everyone recognized the well-known stride of the President of the Church. He was getting older, but he still had a spring in his step. He waved to the crowd, and Carol couldn't hold back her tears as she watched the screen.

The prophet stepped to the podium. "Good morning, my dear brothers and sisters. You seem a bit surprised to see me!"

The crowd laughed, and he continued, "I'm grateful to the good brethren who helped me arrive here. We had a couple of close calls, but the Lord protected us, and I'm honored to be among you."

He then explained that the meeting would serve as the General Conference of the Church, and his message would be broadcast to gatherings of the Saints across the world.

"That's us," Denise said, smiling up at Carol.

The prophet stepped aside briefly as a local Church leader gave an opening prayer, and then the prophet spoke again.

"Today I speak to you at the base of the majestic Manti Temple, built by faithful Latter-day Saints more than a century ago," he told the worldwide audience. "Those early Saints faced many struggles, but they overcame them and gave us this remarkable building as their legacy.

"At this time, it is our opportunity to create our own legacy on a much larger scale. We are the privileged generation that will build Zion, even the New Jerusalem. Each of you who are listening to my voice have been put through many trials over the past few months, yet you have stayed faithful. In order to create a Zion people, the Lord has put us through a sifting process. We all have friends, and even family members, who were considered active members of the Church just a year ago, but who are no longer a part of us. For whatever reason, they have chosen a different path.

"These trials haven't been easy, but they have prepared us for what lies ahead. I assure you that the troubles are far from over, but I also assure you that the Savior Jesus Christ is carefully watching over the members of this Church.

"We are now in the midst of a worldwide crisis that has long been prophesied. Do not despair. The very fact you are members of this Church at this crucial time in history shows that in the premortal world you were valiant children of our Heavenly Father. Now you are on the earth to help prepare the way for the Second Coming of our Lord."

The prophet cleared his throat, and then took on a glow as if heaven itself was shining down on him.

"The Church is in excellent shape and is functioning at full capacity. In these dangerous times, each of the apostles have spread out to serve in various ways throughout the world. We are like those first apostles of this dispensation called by Joseph Smith. We may be separated by distance, but we are united in purpose. By spreading out, we are assured that the proper priesthood keys will always be on the earth. The death of one of us will not cause the loss of these keys, since members of the First Presidency and the Quorum of the Twelve all hold the keys of this dispensation.

"If a member of the Quorum of the Twelve dies, another worthy man will be ordained to the quorum. In fact, the day will soon come when the Quorum of the Twelve will reunite. That will be a joyous day. But until that time, we will serve throughout the world proclaiming this gospel."

The prophet concluded by bearing his testimony of the truthfulness of the gospel and the latter-day work that was taking place. He promised the Saints that their current distress would only be for a short time. Then Zion's banner would be unfurled for all the world to see.

Following a closing prayer, the prophet waved to the crowd, and the broadcast ended. As the screen went dark, a powerful dose of the Holy Spirit descended on the pavilion, and Carol felt like her breath was taken away. Everyone sat still for several seconds before stirring in their seats. Most of the group, both men and women, were wiping away tears as they began to converse.

"Why is everyone crying?" Denise asked. "I feel very happy."

"Well, that's the reason," Carol said. "We're happy to hear the prophet of the Lord tell us we're on the right track. We are getting closer to becoming a Zion people."

Throughout the rest of the day a holy aura filled the camp. Carol could sense a difference. They had been living righteously, but the prophet's message had elevated them another step higher. She knew that her fellow Saints felt recharged and ready to face whatever may await them.

CHAPTER 17

That night Garrett sat in the new U.N. headquarters in Copperton, an LDS church building located next to the City Park on the southern edge of the town. The church was within sight of the park's tennis courts, now known as the holding pen for prisoners. Plus, the church's parking lot worked great for parking the U.N.'s large transporters.

Garrett tried to block out of his mind how wrong it was for the U.N. soldiers to be tromping through the church building. It was just another aspect of daily life where everything had been turned upside down and God had been forgotten.

They were sitting in the chapel, where images from around the world were being projected on a big screen. Commander Klopov and thirty other men surrounded Garrett as they watched reports of the full-scale Coalition invasion that had begun that day on both U.S. coasts.

The reports were a mixture of satellite images and actual video footage recorded by soldiers on the ground. The videos included audio clips from Coalition leaders praising their forces. They had expected at least some kind of military opposition, but it looked like it was going to be a cakewalk to occupy the country.

"We should have done this years ago," one Coalition leader proclaimed.

Even though the Coalition was completely confident of victory, they wanted to keep the cities intact for their own citizens to move into once the invasion was over. So they had begun the attack by firing a few conventional missiles into major cities. The goal was to terrify the American citizens and send them scurrying inland like mice, where they could be rounded up and exterminated.

Garrett tried not to openly cringe as he watched several prominent landmarks in Los Angeles and New York City get bombarded by explosives. Several of those cities' tallest skyscrapers were toppled within minutes, showering enormous amounts of rubble onto the streets.

Klopov laughed next to him as footage showed frightened U.S. citizens running away from the explosions. "Look at those American crybabies," he said, giving Garrett a nudge in the ribs. "You must be glad not to be one of them anymore."

The scenes soon shifted to images of Coalition ships docking at several ports. Thousands of Coalition soldiers rushed into the cities, all dressed in their distinctive light-colored uniforms and armed with high-powered rifles and small swords. As the soldiers moved inland, they showed no mercy, using their swords to viciously cut down any American they came across, no matter whether it was a man, woman or child. The soldiers had been told to save their ammunition for later, in case they met any real resistance.

The U.N. soldiers around Garrett howled with delight as they watched the barbaric attacks. They were treating it as just another night at the movies. Garrett couldn't watch anymore.

"I'll be back in a while," Garrett told Klopov.

The Russian gave him a smile. "Is it too much for you?"

"I'll be okay," Garret said. "I just need some fresh air."

He walked outside of the church and went behind a bush, where he threw up. His whole body trembled in disgust. The images had been horrific, and the worst part was they were real. It wasn't the latest Hollywood production being shown on that screen. It was his fellow U.S. citizens being killed.

He walked a few more steps then fell face first on the grass.

"Heavenly Father, please help me escape from this awful situation," Garrett prayed. "I can't take it anymore. I'm surrounded by barbarians. I'd rather die than endure much more of this."

He lay there for several minutes in the dark, and then a warmth filled his chest and he heard the word, "*Soon.*"

Garrett looked up, but no one was around, but he audibly heard "*Soon*" once again.

"Thank thee, Heavenly Father," Garrett cried. "I will be patient."

❧

The next morning Garrett was back on duty sorting out the recently captured prisoners. It was the usual mix of Salt Lake residents who felt somehow entitled to special treatment.

One man really grated on Garrett's nerves as he talked about his multi-level marketing company. He then explained how his leadership skills would be invaluable in rebuilding America to its former greatness.

Garrett shook his head. "I've got news for you. America was invaded yesterday by foreign armies. Your life will never be the same. They'll be here in Utah within days."

The man looked shocked. "That can't be right. God will protect this land."

"I'm sorry, but America turned away from God. Please go get on the bus."

As the day progressed, Garrett's mood continued to grow sour. Then another prisoner slowly approached the table. Garrett glanced up at a middle-aged man with a week's worth of facial hair and several scrapes on his arms.

Garrett's U.N. colleague handed him a paper and said, "This is a special case. He was picked up near the mountains by a helicopter team. He doesn't have a chip. It looks like he cut it out."

Aaron kept his head bowed as Garrett looked at the report.

"You don't have a chip," Garrett said. "I could order your immediate death. Hey, look at me when I speak to you!"

Aaron looked up, and Garrett knew those eyes. He involuntarily recoiled as a tangible shock passed through him. *Aaron Shaw? Was it possible?*

"Please spare my life, sir," Aaron said contritely. "I'm willing to cooperate with you."

"What skills do you have?" Garrett asked.

"I'm a computer guy," Aaron said. "Maybe you already have a bunch of those types, but I think I'm different."

Garrett looked at him thoughtfully. "Yes, we shouldn't let your talents go to waste."

The two spontaneously smiled at each other. The other U.N. officer watched the exchange and could tell something unusual was going on. Garrett hadn't smiled all day, not even at a beautiful brunette woman who had tried to flirt with him a few minutes earlier. He had simply ordered her to get on the bus.

"We need to eliminate this man," the U.N. officer told Garrett as he pointed at Aaron. "I sense trouble."

Garrett looked at the U.N. soldier, and then back at Aaron, who had bowed his head and was staring at the ground.

"No, he could be valuable to us," Garrett responded. "Let's lock him up in the outer barracks for now. I want to question him again once we settle in for the night."

CHAPTER 18

The past several hours had been a whirlwind for the Fosters and the Smiths. Elder Smith had given his wife a powerful healing blessing, and she had bounced back almost instantaneously. She said her arm had never felt better.

Meanwhile, Nathan had been discussing with the temple guard the best route to reach Rexburg. During the "old days" prior to the earthquake, it was possible to drive from Bountiful to Rexburg in about three hours. Now there were obstacles on every side, and even getting there within a week seemed unlikely.

The biggest problems were that the Great Salt Lake now filled many of the lower valley areas, and the mountains were more formidable than ever after dozens of landslides had cascaded down the slopes. Their only hope was to move along the foothills and trust that the Lord would open a way for them.

It was finally decided that two large four-wheelers decked out in camouflage was the best option. They also wore camouflage clothing, because they would be passing near Hill Air Force Base between Layton and Ogden. The base was clearly operational, based on the number of helicopters coming from that direction each day. If they got spotted, it would be the end for all four of them. The goal was to pass the military base during the night and then navigate the streets of Ogden during the day.

Due to the frail nature of the Smiths, it was decided that Nathan would drive one four-wheeler with Elder Smith on back, and Marie would drive the other one, accompanied by Sister Smith.

They got a decent night's sleep in the temple, then they departed early the next morning. Just before they left, Marie asked, "Elder Smith, would you please give me a blessing? I know the Lord will watch over us, but I'm going to need some divine help steering this beast of a machine."

"I would be honored," Elder Smith said. "Would you like to receive one as well, Nathan?"

"Certainly," he said.

After the two blessings, Elder Smith shook Nathan's hand and said, "Now it's my turn."

Nathan was taken by surprise as the apostle turned and settled into the seat he had just vacated. "You want me to give you a blessing?" he asked.

Elder Smith smiled. "Yes, I'd be deeply grateful if you would do so."

Nathan swallowed hard, then moved behind the apostle and placed his hands on Elder Smith's head. He offered a silent prayer, and then as he pronounced the blessing, the words flowed from somewhere beyond him, as if a conduit had opened to heaven. He concluded by promising Elder Smith that his life would be preserved until his mission on earth was complete.

After the blessing, Elder Smith clutched Nathan's shoulders with both hands and said, "Well done. I really needed that."

❧

The first stretch of the journey went more smoothly than expected. After the earthquake, other travelers had made decent trails along existing roads in the foothills east of Centerville and Farmington. They connected up with U.S. Highway 89 east of Kaysville and made pretty good time, despite a few cracks in the road. They discovered that the earthquake damage was less horrific the farther north they went from the epicenter. This helped them achieve their goal of getting within range of Hill Air Force Base by nightfall.

When they were nearly past Layton, Nathan motioned for

Marie to follow him, and they pulled off the road and parked behind a vacant home.

"We all need a rest," Nathan said. "Let's save our strength for tonight when we sneak past Hill Air Force Base."

Sister Smith nodded tiredly. "I didn't know it could be so tiring to just ride along, but I'm exhausted! You're doing an incredible job, Marie."

"Thank you," Marie said. "There were only a couple of times I nearly sent us flying down a ravine."

They opened the packs of food they had brought with them, and they ate quietly, savoring the quiet surroundings.

Elder Smith looked at Marie and decided it was finally time to tell her what had happened to her father Aaron. He had nearly told her about him several times while they were still at the Bountiful Temple, but each time the Spirit restrained him from doing so. It now felt like the appropriate time.

"Marie, you have a wonderful father," Elder Smith said.

Marie's eyes brightened. "You know my father? He never told me that you had met."

Elder Smith gave a sad smile. "It was just recently, while I was at the Salt Lake Temple after the earthquake. He arrived at the temple with Elder Bushman of the Seventy to share with the General Authorities some information about the NSA. He was very helpful."

"Where is he now?" Marie asked urgently. "I really want to see him."

"That's the problem. He and I followed the same path you and Nathan did over the ridge into Bountiful just a few days ago, but as we got near the temple, an Army helicopter spotted him and took him away. I feel he distracted them on purpose so I wouldn't be captured."

There was an awkward silence, then Elder Smith added, "I'm sorry I didn't tell you earlier, but I felt it might have caused you to stay behind and search for him. I have prayed night and day that he will be protected."

Marie wiped tears from her eyes. "It's okay. You're right. I probably would have tried to save him."

Nathan put his arms around her. "Thank you for telling us. It's a relief to finally hear what had happened to him. We had stopped by the house in Orem for any signs of him, but it was like he had vanished."

"He told me about his experiences after the earthquake," Elder Smith said. "He was driving to work when it struck, and he walked to the NSA Center, but there was all kinds of trouble going on. So he cut out his chip and started walking toward Temple Square. He finally ended up at Elder Bushman's home, and they made their way through the floodwaters to the temple. He was a great help to me. I would have never made it to Bountiful without him."

Marie nodded sadly. "I just hope I get to see him again."

CHAPTER 19

Back in Copperton, the U.N. peacekeepers ate their dinner in the church's cultural hall, where they had discovered a nice collection of tables and folding chairs to use.

As they finished eating, Commander Klopov invited everyone to enjoy another night of watching the Coalition's destruction of America.

"There's not much we can do for another couple of days," he told them. "We've been ordered to take control of Salt Lake City, but the floodwaters are still too high. So let's watch our comrades again tonight. Aren't they doing a great job?"

Garrett joined them at the beginning, mainly to see whether the Americans were putting up any resistance. He sat near the back of the chapel this time, rather than next to Klopov. Garrett had other plans for the evening.

After watching a few minutes of footage showing yet another roundup of frightened, unprepared Americans, Garrett slipped out of the building. He walked across the street to the tennis courts, where a lone guard was standing. The soldier snapped to attention when Garrett approached.

"At ease, soldier," Garrett told him. "Are these prisoners giving you any trouble?"

"No," the soldier said. "One of the men tried to climb the fence, but I shot him down. He's the one whimpering over there in the corner."

Garrett peered through the fence and saw a young man curled up in a ball holding his bloody shoulder. The rest of the prisoners were standing at the far end of the enclosure, as far from the guard as possible.

"Excellent," Garrett said. "At least they know who is in control."

The soldier beamed. "Thank you, sir. I'm doing my best."

Garrett put his hand on the soldier's arm. "Hey, you know what? You deserve a break. Everyone else is in there watching the footage of the invasion. I'm kind of bored with it. I'll take your spot while you go get something to eat."

"Really? You'd do that for me?"

"Well, Klopov would probably get angry about it, but if you come back quickly, everything should be fine."

"Thank you, sir," the soldier said, handing Garrett his rifle. "I'll be back in ten minutes."

Garrett watched the solider jog across the street and enter the church. Then he turned to the tennis courts and shouted, "Shaw! Get over here right now!"

He saw a figure approaching him in the fading sunlight, and soon Aaron stood on the other side of the fence.

"Hello, my friend," Garrett said quietly. "Get down on your knees and go with the flow. We've got about nine minutes to talk."

As Aaron kneeled down, Garrett suddenly shouted, "I'm not messing around! If you don't tell me where your family is, you're going to the pit!"

Aaron looked up cautiously, not sure if Garrett was acting or not, but Garrett winked at him and whispered, "I've gotta keep everyone at bay. You were able to track our family members when you were working at the NSA Center, right?"

"Yes."

"Then tell me what you know."

Aaron stared at the ground and said, "Well, are you aware that your wife Vanessa is listed as dead?"

"Yes, we were in Pasadena and both got sick. I somehow survived, but I figured she didn't."

"How did you end up with the United Nations?"

"I made my way to Long Beach and got captured, then I

went through this same process. They needed my skills, and I miraculously climbed the ranks."

"That's incredible," Aaron said.

"Enough about me," Garrett said. "What else do you know about my kids?"

"I believe Nathan and Marie are alive and together. He went to rescue her in Chicago, and she cut out her chip while she was there. So I wasn't able to track them anymore, but I feel they're okay."

"What about Denise? Is she with Carol?"

"I think so," Aaron said. "Things were getting pretty bad in Orem, so we staged their deaths. They took off up Provo Canyon to go to a Church camp near Kamas. But then the big earthquake struck. I hope they made it safely before the two dams broke. I've been on the run myself after the quake, so I haven't tracked them since."

"Okay," Garrett said. "I'm going to see what I can do to get you out of here. Don't do anything stupid like climbing the fence. Keep a low profile. Now get back to the group before the guard returns."

Aaron nodded and got to his feet without even looking at Garrett.

"You're a liar!" Garrett shouted at him. "Get back with the others before I kill you!"

Aaron quickly walked back to the cluster of other prisoners, just before the U.N. guard hurried out of the church and rejoined Garrett.

"That was fast," Garrett said. "Did you get enough to eat?"

"Yes, sir. I didn't want to be late."

"Thank you," Garrett said, handing him back the rifle. "You're doing a great job."

Garrett walked back to the church, but instead of returning to the chapel, he entered the small classroom that served as his private sleeping quarters. The room was dark, which matched Garrett's mood. He was sick of his situation, but he felt trapped. He surprised himself by shutting the door, then kneeling down and spontaneously praying once again.

"Heavenly Father, thank thee for connecting me with Aaron, and please watch over him. He made it sound like our family members are still alive."

A warm feeling filled Garrett's chest, a sensation he hadn't experienced in a long time.

"Thank thee, Heavenly Father. If it be thy will, allow me to free Aaron. He doesn't deserve to die here."

The warm feeling continued, and Garrett lowered his head to the floor and wept.

CHAPTER 20

The Smiths and the Fosters had quietly worked their way past Hill Air Force Base during the midnight hour without drawing attention to themselves. They had stayed on a dirt trail in the midst of some trees that hid them well. Thankfully there were aircraft flying in and out of the base even at that hour, and the noise the jets created easily disguised the four-wheeler engines.

"That sure is a busy place," Elder Smith said to Nathan as they got back onto U.S. 89 and climbed the hill to South Ogden. "I wonder if things have gotten worse along the coasts."

They made their way up to the foothills above Ogden to avoid anyone in the city. The moon was nearly full, and the dirt paths seemed to stand out clearly to Nathan and Marie as they drove the four-wheelers steadily northward.

By sunrise they were exhausted. They had been riding almost constantly for a full 24 hours. Sister Smith held on tightly to Marie, but she nearly fell off a few times as sleep overcame her.

When they reached the upper streets of North Ogden, Marie pulled alongside Nathan and called out, "We need to stop!"

He nodded and pointed to an overgrown yard with several bushes. They parked behind the bushes, and everyone dismounted.

"I'm sorry," Sister Smith said. "My old bones are aching, and I can hardly stay awake."

Elder Smith took her in her arms. "I'm feeling the same way. We need to take a break."

"I do too," Marie said. "It is going to take us a few days to get to Rexburg. We need to pace ourselves."

Nathan went to the home on the yard and peered inside the front window. There were no signs of life, and things were scattered everywhere as if the occupants had left in a hurry. He tried the front door, and it wasn't even latched.

"Let me check this place out," he told the others. "Maybe we can rest in here."

He walked cautiously through the home. It looked like anything electronic like TVs or desktop computers were missing, but there were three queen-sized beds still in the home.

The others had joined him inside, and Nathan told the Smiths, "Check for bedbugs, but go ahead and take a long nap. You too, Marie. I'll keep watch for a while, then we'll trade off."

The others didn't hesitate at his offer.

Once they were asleep, Nathan walked out to the road and looked down the slope. He shook his head. The Great Salt Lake had flooded up against I-15, and judging by the water level, it wasn't going to get any better heading north to Brigham City.

Just then he saw a curious sight about a mile away. In the water along the freeway there was a small motorboat heading south.

"Catch up to it."

The voice was audible, and Nathan wondered if his sleep-deprived condition was making him hear voices.

"Catch it now! "

"Okay," Nathan said. "I get the message."

He looked at the nearby street sign so he'd know how to get back to the house, then he jumped on a four-wheeler and headed down the slope toward the boat. He was in such a hurry that he nearly rolled it on one turn, but he managed to shift his weight just in time.

As he got closer to the water, he lost sight of the boat and briefly panicked, but as he made a final turn, he saw the boat pulling up to a patch of dry land.

A dark-haired young man waved his arms, and Nathan stopped the four-wheeler. To his surprise, he recognized the boat operator. He walked over and said, "Dallin Reed? Are you still on duty?"

"Aren't we all?" Dallin said with grin as they shook hands. "It's good to see a fellow maintenance missionary again."

They had been together in Elder Miller's first "MM" orientation meeting in the Joseph Smith Building and had worked together in distributing thousands of tents to the various mountain camps.

"Are you just out fishing today?" Nathan asked. "Getting any bites?"

Dallin laughed. "No. As part of my assignment, I help people get through this next stretch where the lake has flooded everything."

"I wondered about that," Nathan said.

"Yeah, it's pretty bad. Once you get around this hill, there's no way to get across those mountains except by hiking, and they are mighty steep. So I cruise along here every other day to see if someone needs help. You'd be surprised how many stragglers are still trying to find safety. When I saw you burning rubber down the hill, I didn't know if you were a friend or a foe, but I thought I better find out what was so urgent."

"Well, your timing is perfect, because I do have some pretty important people taking a nap up there on the hill—Elder Smith of the Quorum of the Twelve and his wife, along with my wife. We need to help them get to Rexburg."

Dallin raised his eyebrows. "You have a wife? How did you manage that? If I recall, we were all single when we got set apart as maintenance missionaries."

Nathan laughed. "It's a long story, but it's all approved by the Church leaders."

Dallin shook his head and smiled. "Some guys have all the luck. Anyway, let's get going. We can take this boat almost to the mouth of Sardine Canyon, then I've got a truck we can use to get you to Cache Valley."

"Is that the fastest way to Rexburg?" Nathan said.

"No, but it's the safest route. The junction of I-15 and I-84 near Tremonton is basically a haven for robbers. They prey upon anyone who passes that way. I've heard a few terrible stories from people who survived their attacks."

"I'm glad you told me," Nathan said. "I would've led us right into their hands."

Dallin looked at the boat's fuel gauge. "I'm getting low on gas, but I have a hidden stash a few miles farther south. If you want to meet me back here with the others in about an hour, that should work."

"We'll be here."

The two friends shook hands again, then Nathan got on the four-wheeler and hurried back up the hill. He went in the house and gently shook Marie awake.

"I'm sorry to cut your nap so short," he said, "but we need to go now."

Marie sat up with a start. "Is everything okay?"

"Yes. The Lord is watching out for us."

They awakened the Smiths, and Nathan explained how Dallin was going to take them to Cache Valley.

"What a blessing," Sister Smith replied. "This isn't reflection on your driving, Marie, but the Lord knew I couldn't take many more miles on that four-wheeler."

"No offense taken," Marie said. "I won't miss it either."

"Well, it's just one more short ride down the hill, then we'll have to leave the machines behind," Nathan said. "Let's go. Dallin will be there soon."

⁂

Dallin returned to their meeting place just as they arrived, and they transferred their packs from the four-wheelers to the boat. Dallin helped the Smiths into the boat while Nathan and Marie parked the vehicles in an old shed that was nearby so Dallin could use them in the future if needed.

It turned out Dallin and the Smiths had several common acquaintances in the Brigham City area. Soon it was like they were old friends. Then Dallin settled into the business of navigating the boat through a maze of underwater obstacles.

"I've figured out my route pretty well now," he said, "but my first trip down here took several hours. I kept running aground on submerged cars and fences."

They made their way north, and Nathan noticed that the Great Salt Lake's dikes against the freeway had indeed broken. Many of the homes in the town of Perry were half-submerged, and the boat startled quite a few ducks and other waterfowl as it motored along through town.

As they approached Brigham City later in the day, Sister Smith pointed ahead. "See the temple? It looks as good as ever."

"Yes, most of Brigham City lucked out and stayed dry, thanks to being on the ridge," Dallin said. "Now it's like a peninsula."

He looked at the afternoon sun, then added, "There's no point in staying here overnight if we can reach Logan before nightfall."

He steered the boat toward the south end of Brigham City, and they reached land within sight of an auto dealership.

"I just park my truck in the midst of all these other vehicles, and no one bothers it," he said, leading them to a white truck.

They moved their packs from the boat to the truck, then took a few minutes to eat. Dallin turned to Elder Smith and asked, "So everything regarding the Church is shifting north for now, right?"

"What do you mean?" Elder Smith asked.

"Well, we've all seen firsthand that these valleys are pretty much uninhabitable right now. It is going to take a major effort to clean things up even if the water drops, which isn't happening very quickly."

"You're right," the apostle said. "The Lord foresaw what was going to happen, and the Church has been preparing Rexburg for several years to be the temporary headquarters of the Church."

"What do you mean by a 'temporary' headquarters?" Marie asked. "Rexburg isn't going to get destroyed too, is it?"

"No," Elder Smith said. "Rexburg will become a wonderful City of Light with thousands of Saints living there. What I mean by temporary is that it will be the main base of the Church until Missouri is fully cleansed and we can establish New Jerusalem."

"That makes sense," Marie said. "But Rexburg? Who would've ever thought of it?"

They all chuckled as Sister Smith added, "We're hoping the invading armies will feel the same way. If we're lucky—and with the Lord's blessing and protection—they will completely ignore it."

Soon Dallin was driving them up Sardine Canyon. Elder and Sister Smith sat with him in the cab, while Nathan and Marie rode in the back of the truck. They enjoyed cuddling together on some cushions they had found inside the auto dealership.

"I sure do love you," Nathan told her. "I wouldn't want to share this adventure with anyone else."

She leaned up, kissed him hard, and said, "Same to you."

A few miles up the canyon, they reached a checkpoint that was manned by members of the Church. Dallin gave them the password, then pointed to his passengers. The guards recognized Elder Smith and quickly waved them through.

Within an hour, they entered Cache Valley, and they all looked in wonderment as seemingly half the valley was filled with white tents. They passed an area near the main highway where several groups of men were setting up even more blocks of tents.

"Elder Smith told me the smaller mountain camps had recently been asked to come to the larger valleys," Nathan said to Marie as they peered out of the back of the truck. "That's why everything is in such a frenzy."

Nathan noticed the tents weren't being set up haphazardly. Each field had been marked off in a giant grid using long strings, and the tents were being erected right along those strings. They were all the same distance apart as well.

"It's nice to see how organized everything is," he told Marie. "It reminds me of the stories of the pioneers. Even in times of trouble, there was a sense of order in all they did."

As they passed, the men would pause and wave to them, and they waved back.

"It still amazes me how happy and upbeat everyone is, even after all that we've been through," Marie said.

"I think it's because we feel a sense of purpose," Nathan said. "We're all helping build Zion in our own way."

Marie looked thoughtful. "How are they able to live here without being spotted by the government? You'd think those jets flying out of Hill Air Force Base would easily spot these tents."

"I've thought about that too," Nathan said. "For one thing, I've noticed the jets and helicopters aren't flying over the mountains. They seem to stay on the western side of the Wasatch Front. I watched their flight patterns, and I'm guessing they are flying to the West Coast."

"I agree, but it has to be more than that," Marie said. "I feel the Lord is protecting us in ways we don't even realize."

"You're right. I feel these valleys have a spiritual shield over them. I know the government would love to find us, but through our faith and prayers, they haven't been able to so far."

❧

Dallin soon pulled the truck into the parking lot of the Logan Temple, and they were greeted by several people, including a few members of the Quorums of the Seventy.

As they were led into the temple, Marie and Sister Smith put their arms around each other as they walked.

"I don't know about you," Sister Smith said, "but I'm ready to finish that nap your husband interrupted earlier today."

"Absolutely," Marie said, and within an hour both couples were tucked away in a nearby house for a much-needed night's sleep.

CHAPTER 21

Garrett awoke early, knowing that if he was going to free Aaron, it had to be soon. Commander Klopov had sent a group of peacekeepers to check on the water levels in downtown Salt Lake, and they reported that the flooding had noticeably decreased in the past week.

Klopov was pleased at the news, because he wanted to occupy Temple Square as a symbolic gesture by the time the Coalition forces arrived from the West Coast. He intended to send a portion of their convoy into downtown Salt Lake in a couple of days, and he had appointed Garrett to lead that group.

Garrett was still struggling with how the U.N. troops had desecrated Copperton's LDS chapel. After that experience, he just couldn't lead the way in soiling the Salt Lake Temple and the other buildings on Temple Square. So although he had initially planned on simply freeing Aaron, the impression kept coming that he needed to free himself too. He hadn't necessarily felt trapped until that moment, but now the reality of the situation pressed down upon him.

Garrett left the church building and crossed the street. He nodded to the guard, then walked along the tennis court's fencing. He made eye contact with Aaron, who was standing alone in the middle of the enclosure.

Garrett reached into his pocket and pulled out a note he had written the night before. He briefly held it up for Aaron to see, then he stuck it into the chainlink fence. Garrett then turned without saying a word and headed back to the church for breakfast.

Aaron kept his eye on the note. It didn't appear that any of
the other prisoners had noticed what Garrett had done. He slowly
made his way over to the note, then in one swift motion grabbed
it and clutched it in his hand. A couple of the other prisoners were
now glancing at him, so he just slowly walked the perimeter of the
enclosure for a few minutes until they stopped watching him. He
finally sat down and leaned against the fence, then smoothed out
the note against his leg. It read:

Tonight.
I will cut fence.
We leave in red jeep.
Swallow note.

Aaron felt a wave of relief pass over him. He knew Garrett was
risking everything to help save him, and he was grateful.

He folded the note carefully, then plopped it into his mouth
and started chewing the paper.

❧

The Coalition invasion was proceeding rapidly from both coasts,
particularly through the southeastern United States. It was exciting
to watch, and thankfully Klopov and the other peacekeepers were
completely engrossed by the continual destruction and killing.

This allowed Garrett some free time. He walked behind the
church and checked on a red jeep parked there. When the U.N.
forces had arrived in Copperton, he had immediately noticed the
jeep. It seemed unusual for a nice new vehicle to be parked by itself.

That first day he had hopped inside the jeep and was surprised
to find the key still in the ignition. He had started it up, and it
ran perfectly. He pocketed the key and locked the doors, planning
to use it if Klopov needed him to check other areas. The jeep was
certainly more manageable to drive than the five-axel transporters
they had arrived in.

Now Garrett hoped it would be the perfect getaway vehicle.

Next he went to the church kitchen and loaded two duffel bags with food and water. No one even noticed when he carried them out and put them in the jeep.

Now all he needed was a tool to quietly cut the fence that night. He went to a supply closet and searched high and low for anything that would cut through wire. Then he moved a box of garbage bags and found just what he was looking for. A sturdy bolt cutter.

"That should do the trick," he said to himself. He carried the tool out to the jeep and put it under the duffel bags in the backseat. Then he casually walked back into the chapel and sat down next to Klopov, who was watching Atlanta being ransacked.

"How is the invasion going?" Garrett asked.

"Wonderfully," Klopov replied. "We better send your team to Temple Square tomorrow. We might have some of the Coalition forces here in the valley by the end of the week, and we want to impress them."

"Sounds great," Garrett said. "I look forward to it."

❧

That evening Klopov called a meeting to organize the Temple Square takeover, and Garrett fully participated in the planning. They would take four of the transporters and systematically work their way toward the temple. One of the leaders mentioned that the Mormons might have left a few armed guards behind to protect the temple, but Klopov openly scoffed at that.

"We have enough firepower to turn that temple to dust," he said. "Not that we plan to, because we want to keep historic buildings like that intact. I mean, wouldn't that building make a nice headquarters for me?"

The others in the room smiled and applauded. Then Klopov turned to Garrett and said, "Of course, that doesn't mean you can't eliminate any opposition you might encounter."

"Don't worry, we won't hesitate to do so," Garrett said.

After the meeting, everyone went to their respective sleeping quarters. Garrett lay down on his cot, but he couldn't stop shaking. It felt like he was having a panic attack. Doubts keep creeping into his head.

"Life with the U.N. isn't so bad," he told himself. "And who cares about Aaron? Yes, we are friends, but is it worth giving up everything I have worked for just to set him free?"

Then a memory of Nathan and Denise happily sitting together at their home in Orem earlier that year filled his mind. They were laughing and smiling, and Garrett felt a deep longing to be with his family.

He reminded himself that none of this other stuff mattered at all. Even if he someday rose to great prominence in the Coalition, it would never fill the void of being separated from his family. He knew Aaron was the key to seeing them again.

He stood up and looked around the classroom. There wasn't anything there that he wanted to take with him. He made sure he had the key to the jeep in his pocket, and then he carefully opened the classroom door. Klopov had ordered the building's portable electric generators be turned off at 11 p.m., so he wasn't surprised the hallway was dark.

Garrett quietly closed his door then briskly walked out of the closest exit. His heart was beating wildly, but he kept a steady pace as he walked through the dark to the jeep. The area was silent, and he realized the jeep's engine might alert a guard that something was amiss.

So he changed his plans. Rather than drive to the tennis courts, he would free Aaron first. He grabbed the bolt cutter and headed toward the tennis courts, quietly bypassing where the guard stood and going to the opposite side of the enclosure.

He raised the bolt cutter and began clipping the chainlink at about eye level, then working his way down. Aaron had spotted him and was slowly wandering in his direction.

Within a minute Garrett had sliced open the fence all the way to the ground, and he pulled it back so that Aaron could slip through. They didn't say a word as Garrett took hold of Aaron's wrist and led him through the dark to where the jeep was parked.

Once they were inside the jeep, Garrett still felt the need to whisper.

"We've made it this far, but I'm afraid the engine is going to rile up the guards. We might get shot at if we go through town, but earlier today I noticed we can drive down this ravine."

Aaron looked at the drop-off beyond the edge of the parking lot. "Down there? In the dark?"

"It's our only chance. The main entrances to town are heavily guarded."

Garrett then fished in the jockey box and pulled out a small knife, a mini flashlight, and a first aid kit.

"First things first," he said, handing the knife to Aaron and shining the light on his right hand. "Please get this chip out of me."

Aaron squirmed a little. "I didn't mind cutting out my own, but . . ."

"Just do it," Garrett said a bit testily. "We don't have time to waste."

Aaron got right to work, feeling the little bump on the back of Garrett's hand, then slicing the flesh quickly and using the knife to dislodge the chip. Garrett only gave a small cry of pain as Aaron pinched the chip between his fingers and popped it free from the tissue holding it in place.

"I got it," Aaron said. "What should I do?"

"Smash it," Garrett said.

Aaron took the flashlight and opened the door. He put the chip on the pavement, then took a chunk of broken asphalt and pulverized it.

"Good job," Garrett said as he put a Band-Aid over the cut. "Let's get out of here."

He started the engine but left the lights off. The moon provided just enough illumination for them to find the steep dirt road leading to the ravine. They bumped across a set of railroad tracks, then got onto a better gravel road.

Within a minute they had left Copperton in their dust. After about a mile they connected with the Old Bingham Highway, and Garrett let out a whoop of relief.

"I can't believe we did it!" Aaron said. "Next stop, Kamas."

CHAPTER 22

Commander Klopov had only been awake for a few minutes when he heard some shouting in the foyer of the church. He threw open his door and shouted, "What is all of the commotion?"

All of the prisoners are gone from the tennis courts," another leader said. "Somehow they cut through the enclosure's fence and escaped."

"Where is the guard in charge?" Klopov said.

"He is outside," the man said. "He said he didn't hear a thing all night, but as the sun arose, the enclosure was empty."

Klopov stepped outside to see the damage for himself. He spotted the guard trying to hold his composure. "I'm sorry, sir. I didn't hear anything."

Klopov simply pointed at him, and another soldier shot the guard dead where he stood. There was zero tolerance for this kind of breach in security.

"We found these by the opening," another soldier said, handing him the bolt cutter. "Someone had to have helped them."

"Is everyone accounted for?" Klopov asked. "I want every soldier out here right now."

The leaders went into the church and began checking every room. Soon the entire group stood before him, except one notable exception—the man who should have been at his side.

"Where's Foster?" Klopov asked. "Has anyone seen him this morning?"

The other soldiers shook their heads.

"That spineless American piece of scum," Klopov snarled. "I

should have seen this coming from him. He must have left on foot with his friends."

One of the soldiers raised his hand. "Sir, do you remember the jeep that was parked behind the building? It's gone."

"The red one? Well, that shouldn't be too hard to spot from the air. Get the helicopter ready. It's time for some target practice."

~

Garrett and Aaron were both feeling emotionally frazzled. The gas gauge had been at "empty" for a while, but they kept going as long as the jeep kept running. They checked a couple of gas stations along the way, but they were abandoned and the pumps didn't work.

It had taken them most of the night over some treacherous roads to get across Salt Lake, but by mid-morning they had made their way a few miles up Parley's Canyon. Aaron had stayed alert through the journey and actually got out of the jeep a few times to guide him through some narrow spots. Despite the damage from the earthquake, people had patched together a makeshift road, filling in the biggest cracks in the pavement with flat rocks and dirt. Smaller cars and minivans would never make it, but the jeep had handled the worst spots fairly well.

As they crested Parley's Summit and began traveling downhill, Garrett said, "We just might make it."

Aaron nodded tiredly. "Yeah, it's a miracle this jeep is still running."

But as they approached the outskirts of Park City, Garrett felt the engine begin to cough, and finally it gave out. They coasted downhill for nearly a mile, but then Garrett pulled the jeep off to the side of the road. He pointed at some houses on the north side of the canyon.

"Maybe we can rest there," he said. They each grabbed a duffel bag and started walking in that direction. They reached one of the homes and knocked, but no one was there. The door was locked, so they broke through a front window and settled in on the couches. They ate some snacks, then were asleep within minutes.

~

Commander Klopov sat in the front passenger seat of the helicopter as they soared over Salt Lake City. He was angry at Garrett, but he was also amused at how easy it was to follow the jeep's route. They had immediately spotted the fresh tire tracks on the dirt road outside of Copperton, and although they had lost the tracks a couple of times, there was so much debris on the roads that they soon found the jeep's path again. After a while it was obvious where Garrett was headed. He was aiming straight for Parley's Canyon.

"Where are you going, my delusional American friend?" Klopov asked. "You'll never get away with this."

Within minutes the helicopter crested the summit of Parley's Canyon, and the red jeep came into view on the side of the freeway. They hovered above it for a moment, but it was clear no one was inside it.

"Put it on the ground," Klopov told the pilot. "He must be hiding nearby."

The helicopter settled on the freeway next to the jeep, and Klopov and another soldier climbed out. Klopov put his hand on the hood of the jeep, and it was still warm.

"He isn't far," Klopov said. "Search the area."

The soldier began using a chip-detector, but nothing was showing up on the screen.

"There's no trace of him," the soldier said.

"I'm sure he cut his chip out, like all the cowards do," Klopov said. "Use your heat scanner and he'll turn up. I'll bet he's in one of these houses."

~

The helicopter's arrival had awakened Garrett and Aaron. They crouched down at the window, peering through the blinds as Klopov and the soldier talked. Then the soldier started walking toward the house while holding a device.

"This isn't good," Garrett said. "I think that thing can track body heat. Go hide in the basement. They might not even know you're with me."

"They'll kill you," Aaron said. "We could run out the back door and get away."

Garrett shook his head. "Maybe this is the way it's supposed to end for me, but one of us needs to survive."

The two men briefly embraced, then Aaron turned and descended the basement stairway.

Garrett opened the door with his hands raised and stepped outside onto the driveway. Klopov and his fellow soldier were about thirty yards away, and the soldier immediately dropped the heat scanner and pulled out a pistol. He aimed it squarely at Garrett's chest.

"Hey, hold on there," Garrett said. "I'm not even armed."

"How do you explain your actions?" Klopov asked. "This is clearly against my orders."

"Commander, I'm sorry. I lost my head. The pressure of leading the group into downtown Salt Lake got to me and I freaked out."

"I don't believe you," Klopov said. "I should have never trusted an American."

Klopov raised his hand, and the soldier fired three quick shots into Garrett's chest.

Garrett winced in pain and looked down to see a rapidly widening circle of blood soak his shirt. He fell to his knees and cried out in agony. Then he fell face-first onto the concrete driveway.

The soldier approached Garrett and turned him over with his boot. It was clear he was dead.

"Leave him," Klopov said. "We have no use for his body. Let the animals eat him."

Klopov turned toward the helicopter, and the pilot was standing nearby holding a camera. He gave a thumbs-up sign and said, "I got all of that on video. We can show the world what happens when you try to outwit Commander Klopov."

The Russian grinned. "No one messes with me."

Aaron was hiding under a desk in the basement when he heard the pistol shots. He instinctively knew Garrett had been killed. Within a couple of minutes he heard the whir of the helicopter blades start up and then fade away, but he stayed put for another ten minutes before leaving the basement. He crept to the front window and could see Garrett's body sprawled out on the driveway in a puddle of blood.

"Oh no," Aaron cried. "This can't be happening."

He found a blanket and took it outside to Garrett's body. He gently straightened his friend's arms and legs. He covered him with the blanket before sitting down next to the body and sobbing.

He looked to the east, and dark clouds were beginning to appear above the mountains. It looked like a powerful storm was on its way.

"*Check the shed.*"

The voice startled Aaron, especially since he was sitting next to a dead body. He even lifted the blanket to check if Garrett had spoken, but he clearly hadn't.

But he knew that voice—the voice of the Spirit. So Aaron scanned the area and saw a small metal shed tucked beneath a pine tree across the street. He walked over to it and slid the door open. Inside was a riding lawnmower and a red plastic gas can. He picked up the can and was surprised to find it was mostly full of gasoline. He carried it to the jeep and emptied the can into the gas tank.

Then he returned to Garrett's body and rolled it up tightly in the blanket.

"We're getting out of here," Aaron told his dead friend.

Aaron dragged the body to the jeep and hoisted it into the back seat just as snow began to fall. The jeep struggled to start, but it finally roared to life, and Aaron continued on down the freeway toward the Kamas camp.

Aaron made it to the junction with Highway 189 and traveled a few more miles toward Kamas, but the snow was accumulating quickly on the pavement and he was having a hard time even seeing where the road was. To the left he could see the empty lake bed where Jordanelle Reservoir had been, but its barren shores were soon covered in snow as well.

"Sheesh, what a bad time to have the blizzard of the century," Aaron said. "This is ridiculous."

He slowed to a stop and turned off the engine to preserve the gasoline. He looked at the mountains around him and realized he didn't even know where the turnoff to the Kamas camp would be. He turned to the only option he had left.

"Heavenly Father, if it be thy will, help me to survive this situation," he prayed. "Please inspire any righteous soul that is able to reach me to do so."

CHAPTER 23

Carol and Denise sat under the pavilion at the Heber Valley Camp with several others and watched the snow fall. They had grown accustomed to a string of warm sunny days, so the storm was not a welcome sight.

They had heard that many of the smaller camps were gathering together at places such as Logan and Manti, but Elder Cluff had been told though the ZOOM system that the members at the Heber Valley Camp would stay there for the foreseeable future.

Carol had been happy with that announcement. She hadn't been looking forward to packing everything up and moving somewhere else. But as she watched the snow fall, she hoped she wasn't going to feel trapped as the snow grew deeper throughout the winter.

"Let's go to our tent and get warm," Carol said to Denise. "It looks like winter is coming in strong this year."

Most nights consisted of an evening devotional or a dance, but everyone seemed in agreement to just go to bed and deal with the effects of the storm in the morning.

They shared a smaller tent where they slept on cots in sleeping bags, and Carol was actually very warm and comfortable, even on this snowy night.

Denise drifted off to sleep quickly, but something was nagging at Carol. She felt off-kilter. She lay awake for a half-hour before deciding to go to the tent temple. It was still only 9:30. There was usually someone there until at least ten o'clock.

She quietly put on a dress and her boots, then pulled on a coat.

Denise was still sleeping peacefully, so Carol slipped out of the tent and walked through the snow to the temple. Just inside the door sat Brother Hunter.

"How are you tonight?" Carol asked him. "Would it be okay if I just came in for a few minutes to meditate and pray?"

"Be my guest," Brother Hunter said. "Everyone else has gone to their tents, but I'll wait here until you're ready to leave."

"Thank you."

Carol went to the Celestial Room and pondered her life. She felt lonely, and she wondered where Aaron could possibly be.

Then a small light began to grow in the corner of the room until suddenly her friend Helen appeared before her. Her glory and radiance was almost overpowering.

"My dear Carol, it's wonderful to see you again," Helen said. "Thank you for being in tune. I needed you to come here tonight."

Carol shrugged. "I just felt uneasy, so I came here."

"I'm glad you did. There has been a tragedy. Your husband Aaron is stuck in the snow on the highway west of where the Jordanelle Reservoir was. If someone doesn't reach him by morning, he will pass away."

"What is he doing there?" Carol asked.

"He is trying to reach you, but he thinks you are at the Kamas camp. Either way, he isn't going to survive without help. Go talk to Elder Cluff. He will know what to do."

"I'll go right now," Carol said frantically.

"There's one other thing," Helen said. "The rescuers need to take a sled and a body bag with them. Farewell for now."

Helen then quickly faded away, and Carol rushed to the temple entrance. "Brother Hunter, I need to find Elder Cluff. Do you know where he might be?"

"I think he's holding a meeting over at the big shop to organize the snow-removal duties."

"Thank you," Carol said before starting to run that direction.

Brother Hunter took her by the arm and asked, "Hey, what happened in there? Are you okay?"

I'll be fine soon enough," she said. "You can close the temple now."

Then she hurried toward the big shop where the four-wheelers and trucks were kept. She was happy to see the lights were on. As she reached the shed and opened the door, she could hear Elder Cluff's voice.

"Elder Cluff?" she called out. "I need to talk with you!"

She saw him crouched over a four-wheeler where he and two other men were attaching a plow blade to the front of the machine.

"Hello, Sister Shaw," he said. "What are you doing out here in the snow?"

Carol paused, not quite sure how to explain it, especially with the other two men there. She knew Paul and his son Jake from when they had rescued her family from the side of the mountain, but she wasn't sure they would believe her story. She glanced in their direction, then said, "Uh, I've had another visit from the other side of the veil."

Elder Cluff nodded. "Please tell us about it. You can trust Paul and Jake. They're used to this kind of thing."

"Okay," Carol said. "Well, Helen Foster just appeared to me while I was in the temple. She said my husband Aaron is trapped in the snow on the highway west of Jordanelle Reservoir. She said if we don't send someone to save him, he'll freeze to death."

"Whoa," Paul said. "It's going to be hard to get to him with this snow."

"I know," Carol said. "Is there anything we can do?"

Elder Cluff looked thoughtful. "We do have a few snowmobiles stashed away for emergencies, and this certainly qualifies as one."

"I would think so," Jake said. "Let's ride!"

Paul frowned and shook his head. "I'm sorry, but I think we'd be better off leaving at sunrise. Going down there in this storm would be really dangerous. Maybe the snow will let off by then, too, and we'd get there just as quickly."

"I think that's a good decision," Elder Cluff said. "Let's have you two get the snowmobiles fueled up and ready to go so you can leave first thing in the morning."

"'I'm so grateful for you," Carol said, wiping tears from her eyes. "Oh, I almost forgot. Helen said to take along a sled and a body bag. She didn't explain why."

The men were silent for a moment, but Paul said, "We'll make sure we do."

Carol returned to her tent, but she couldn't sleep, so she left her bed at 5 a.m. and went to the shop. It was barely light outside, but she could see two snowmobile tracks heading down the road toward the camp's main gate. Now all she could do was wait.

CHAPTER 24

At sunrise, Aaron's head slumped forward and hit the jeep's steering wheel, snapping him awake. He looked at the vehicle's windows and saw they were frosted on the inside from his own breath. His whole body ached from the cold, and he knew he was suffering from hypothermia. He still only wore the shirt, pants, and shoes he had been wearing when Garrett had freed him from the enclosure in Copperton.

As the temperature had dropped during the night, he'd had no choice but to turn on the engine every few minutes to put the heater on, but at 4 a.m. he ran out of gasoline, and the last six hours had been brutally cold.

"I need to move, or I'm just going to fall asleep and never wake up," he told himself. He glanced over his shoulder and confirmed once again that this whole scenario was unfortunately real. The blanket containing Garrett's body was still in the back seat.

He opened the door and was pleased to see the blue sky. Everything else was coated in a blanket of white. He stepped out of the jeep and his feet sank into ten inches of powdery snow. Even if he could get the jeep started again, it would have been too deep and slick to drive safely.

A gust of icy wind went up his shirt, and it shocked his already-fragile system. He dropped to his knees, unable to stand any longer. The snow looked like a fluffy blanket that he could just curl up in and take a long nap.

Paul and Jake made good time across the Heber Valley. The snow actually aided their progress, allowing them to cross over rocky patches and debris left by the earthquake and flooding.

As they climbed the highway toward what remained for the Jordanelle Reservoir dam, Jake spotted a glint of red amidst all of the white that surrounded them.

"Dad, I see the jeep up ahead!"

Paul now saw it too, and they sped toward it. Within five minutes they saw a bearded man kneeling against the jeep. He didn't even acknowledge them as they came to a stop.

"Hello!" Paul called out as he hurried to Aaron's side. "How are you feeling?"

Aaron turned his head and gave them a glassy stare. "Oh, I'm feeling all right. How about you?"

Paul and Jake exchanged worried glances. "He's suffering from hypothermia," Paul said. "See if there are any blankets in the jeep."

Jake went to the jeep and grabbed the blanket in the back seat, but it seemed stuck. He tugged a bit more, and Garrett's head emerged.

"Ewww," Jake said, jumping back. "Uh, Dad, we've got a problem here. There's a body in the back of this jeep."

"That's my friend Garrett," Aaron said sleepily. "He got shot."

Paul motioned to Jake to rejoin him. "Let's get him stabilized, then we'll worry about his friend. But that explains why we were told to bring along the body bag and the sled."

❧

Paul and Jake worked with Aaron for a half hour, getting warm fluids into him and continually talking with him. He bounced back rather quickly, and Paul was relieved that the hypothermia wasn't as severe as he first thought.

"Well, we're going to take you to the Heber Valley Camp," Paul told Aaron. "Your wife Carol is there."

Aaron's face brightened. "Really? I thought she was somewhere above Kamas. I would have never found her."

Jake had finished moving the blanket containing Garrett's body to the sled, and now he and Paul put it into the body bag.

"Who is Garrett?" Jake asked.

"He's an old friend," Aaron said. "We both lived in Orem, but he ended up with the U.N. forces. I don't know the whole story, but he helped me escape. Then the U.N. guys tracked us down and shot him near Park City. I got us this far, but then the snow stopped me."

"Well, I think we're ready to head back to camp," Paul said. "Are you feeling strong enough to hold on and ride behind me?"

"Yes."

"Good. We'll have Jake follow us and pull Garrett's body on the sled."

The temperature remained below freezing, which allowed them to make good time on the snowmobiles and not have to contend with mud and runoff. By early afternoon they were back at the gate of the Heber Valley Camp. They waved to the guards, then drove in front of Carol's tent. She had heard the engines and quickly stepped outside.

There was a man on the back of one of the snowmobiles that had shaggy hair and a beard, but she would know those eyes anywhere.

"Aaron, you're alive!" she cried, and rushed to his side to give him a hug and a kiss.

"You look so beautiful," Aaron told her. "I've missed you so much."

Paul hopped off the snowmobile and helped Aaron to his feet. "He needs to recover for a couple of days," Paul said. "He wouldn't have lasted another night."

Jake had been quietly unhooking the sled from his snowmobile, and Carol noticed for the first time the cargo it held.

"Oh no," she said. "Who is this?"

"Garrett Foster," Aaron said softly.

"Garrett? I don't understand."

Aaron pulled her close. "I'll explain it all to you later. But maybe we need to hold a funeral and bury him before the ground freezes."

"I have Denise here with me," Carol said. "She's over at the pavilion helping prepare dinner. It will be hard to break the news to her. First she lost Vanessa, and now Garrett."

Just then Elder Cluff joined them. "I heard the snowmobiles return," he said. "I hope there's some good news."

"There is," Carol said. "This is my husband Aaron. He needs a good shave, but he's doing all right."

Aaron and Elder Cluff shook hands. "Welcome to the camp. We need every able-bodied priesthood holder we can get."

Elder Cluff's eyes then moved to the body bag on the sled. "Oh, I didn't see this. Is this someone we know?"

"It's Denise's father," Carol said. "Garrett Foster."

Elder Cluff looked surprised and confused. "So this is Nathan Foster's dad?"

"It is."

Elder Cluff shook his head, then looked up at the sky. "This doesn't make any sense. Last night I had a vivid dream of Nathan and his dad helping the Church fight for freedom against the invading forces. I've never met Garrett, but I'm certain it was him."

Elder Cluff stood silently for a few seconds, and so did everyone else, unsure what was going on. Finally Elder Cluff turned to Jake and said, "In which end of the bag is Garrett's head?"

Jake pointed at the far end. "The end with the zipper handle."

Elder Cluff simply nodded, then knelt at the end of the bag and unzipped it about a foot. He looked at the others and said, "Pray in your hearts for a miracle."

He then stuck his hands into the bag and located Garrett's head. He then proclaimed in a loud voice, "Garrett Foster, in the name of the Savior Jesus Christ and by the authority and power of the Melchizedek Priesthood, I command your spirit to reenter your physical body and be made whole!"

Elder Cluff got to his feet, and watched the bag intently. So did everyone else.

Carol gasped as she spotted the bag start to shift slightly. Then a muffled voice came from the bag: "Get me out of here!"

Everyone exhaled at once. Paul and Jake leaped into action. They unzipped the bag and lifted the blanket out. Garrett was struggling to get loose, but Paul said, "Hold on, we're going to free you."

They placed him on the ground and gently unrolled the blanket, finally uncovering a smiling Garrett. Everyone gave cries of happiness and awe.

Garrett stood up and gestured to Elder Cluff. "Are you the one who called me back?"

Elder Cluff nodded. "The Spirit told me your work on earth isn't done. We need you here."

Garrett's eyes got misty. "Thank you so much. I was given a life review while in the Spirit World, and it was terrible. I have failed in so many ways. I'll be a better man now."

Aaron pointed at his blood-stained shirt. "Hey, I have to admit I'd like to see what your gunshot wounds look like now."

Garrett shrugged. "Me too."

He unbuttoned his shirt, and they were all astounded to see what looked like scar tissue where the bullets had entered.

"That's amazing," Aaron said. "You were bleeding heavily just a day ago. So you're feeling okay?"

Garrett nodded happily. "Never better. I'm eager to see Denise. Carol, she's here with you, right?"

"Yes, but I recommend both you and Aaron clean up first."

"That's fine," Garrett said. "I saw some things in the Spirit World that I want to share with you."

❧

Less than an hour later they were in Elder Cluff's large, warm tent. Denise had come running when she heard her father was in the camp, and they had happily embraced. She now sat next to him holding his hand as the others who had witnessed his return from the dead joined them in the tent.

Garrett first told them about his adventures the past few months, beginning with awakening in a Pasadena parking lot, then making his way to Santa Monica before being captured by the U.N. peacekeepers in Long Beach.

They all marveled as he described how he worked his way up the leadership ladder and then traveled to Utah with the U.N. convoy.

"So is the world really that frightening out there?" Paul asked. "We get some reports, but it is hard to picture it."

"It is terrible," Garrett said, "and the Coalition invasion that has just started has been horrific. The reason I decided to leave the U.N. was because my new assignment was to conquer downtown Salt Lake. I just couldn't do it. I decided I would rather die than do so. So I helped Aaron escape, and we tried to make our way here. But they caught up to us, and Commander Klopov didn't hesitate to kill me."

Carol raised her hand. "You said you saw some things in the Spirit World that you wanted to share with us."

"Yes. It was a strange experience. I was greeted by two lovely women, my first wife Helen and also Denise's mother Vanessa. That was kind of scary in itself! I think they wanted to tease me and give me a rough time, but they are such good people they couldn't do it. They admitted they are now very close friends. Helen is an angel in so many ways."

Garrett teared up and could hardly speak. He finally pointed to Carol and said, "Vanessa said you performed her temple work here in the tent temple. She wanted me to thank you."

He continued, "I was then shown a review of my life. I admit it was really tough to watch some parts, and to see in particular how my actions have hurt many people. I was so embarrassed by the stupid things I've done, but I also saw that I was a better person than I remembered. I do have many good qualities."

"You do," Denise said. "You're a wonderful father."

Garrett smiled at her. "Thank you. But as most of you know, I'm not a member of the LDS Church right now, and I knew I was either going to spend eternity alone in the Terrestrial Kingdom, or I needed to make some drastic changes. I pleaded with the man who showed me my life review to give me another chance, but he wasn't too sympathetic. He told me, 'You just got shot in the chest by a high-powered weapon. That's pretty irreversible except by the priesthood.'"

"Well, here you are," Aaron said. "How did you pull it off?"

Garrett smiled, "I glanced at Helen, and she had a determined look in her eye. She said to the man, 'Don't take him anywhere until I get back.' She returned fairly soon and said, 'Permission has been granted, and Aaron has been prompted what he must do.'"

Aaron's eyes widened. "That must have been when I heard a voice tell me to look in the shed. That's where I found the gas for the jeep."

"It was," Garrett said. "At that point, I was shown where Nathan and Marie are. Did you know they got married?"

Carol and Denise nodded happily, but Aaron looked shocked. "Wow. That's great," he said. "Did you see where they are now?"

"Yes, they're on their way to Rexburg. I saw that we need to join them soon."

"How can we do that?" Carol asked. "This snow will make it almost impossible to travel very far."

Garrett looked her in the eye. "I don't know. All I can say is I was dead an hour ago, and now I'm sitting here with you. We'll find a way."

CHAPTER 25

The snowstorm that had hit Heber had moved north overnight and walloped Logan as well. It caught the Fosters and the Smiths by surprise when they awoke. Dallin Reed had left the previous evening to return to his assignment in Brigham City.

"I wish we still had Dallin and his truck here," Marie said. "That thing wouldn't have had any trouble with this snow."

"We'll get to Rexburg somehow," Nathan replied. "Let me find Elder Smith and we'll see what the plan is."

Nathan found Elder Smith talking with Brother Mortensen, a member of the Logan Temple presidency. They spotted Nathan and welcomed him into their conversation.

"We have scouts and spies along all of the roads to Rexburg, and traveling I-15 just isn't a safe route," Brother Mortensen said. "A few weeks ago you could have safely gone straight north from here through Preston and then connected with I-15. But since the earthquake and economic problems, things have changed. There have been shootings and robberies wherever the canyons get narrow, such as in the town of Inkom, and Pocatello isn't much better. You're just so vulnerable to being attacked."

"What do you suggest?" Nathan asked. "Is there another route that won't take us too far out of the way?"

"Yes. I was telling Elder Smith just now that the best route would be up Logan Canyon, then past Bear Lake and over to Star Valley, Wyoming. You could recuperate there before heading north and cutting over to Rigby, Idaho. That route will allow you to bypass Idaho Falls, where there's been reports of trouble."

Nathan turned to Elder Smith and asked, "What do you think?"

The apostle nodded slowly. "I feel good about it. If we can avoid any more storms, we should make pretty good time. I've asked for them to provide us with a four-wheel drive truck. You've driven enough of those white Church box trucks that you shouldn't have any trouble at all, right?"

Nathan smiled. "It should be a piece of cake."

Brother Mortensen said, "We're going to send a snowplow ahead of you, so that should make things a lot easier."

"Then let's get on the road," Elder Smith said. "It honestly feels like I'm living inside one of those bad dreams where you're really late for an important meeting, and you just can't get there."

"Well, that's kind of the truth, isn't it?" Nathan asked.

"Yes. In a way that is hard to describe, my fellow apostles are reaching out to me, and we need each other's steadying influence. I can't wait to see them again."

∼

Eight hours later they reached Star Valley, Wyoming, and they followed the snow plow into a church parking lot in the town of Afton. It had taken them nearly a full day to make a trip that could usually be completed in less than three hours.

There were still a few tents set up on the church grounds, but overall the town was quiet. The valley had been a Place of Refuge during the summer and fall, but most of the Saints had traveled to Logan the previous week to join the larger group there.

The first stretch from Logan to a refueling point near Bear Lake had been tolerable, but as they began the climb through the mountains to Star Valley, the snow was more than two feet deep in some spots, and the snowplow driver ahead of them had struggled to climb to the top of some of the passes. There were several stretches where he barely reached ten miles an hour.

They were in a double-cab truck, with the Fosters in the front and the Smiths in the back seat. Nathan was driving, and he was being very cautious, but more than once the truck started sliding toward the edge of the road where a steep drop-off awaited them. Marie was sure the right-front tire had actually left the road.

"Hey, you're going to get us killed!" she shouted at Nathan. "Keep your eyes on the road!"

"I'm doing my best," Nathan responded. "Sorry."

The same thing happened a couple of more times, though, and each time Marie snapped at him to be more careful.

The Smiths had tried to keep the conversation light after each of Marie's outbursts, but finally everyone settled into silence as Marie fought within herself to avoid a complete emotional breakdown. She had been through many trials during the past year, but the stress of the past few hours ranked right up there with anything else she had experienced.

Marie could tell something wasn't right with her body. When the truck pulled to a stop in Afton, she leaped out and promptly threw up. Sister Smith gently took her by the arm to help her. "Let's see if there's a doctor in the church," she said.

"I'm fine," Marie said. "Just give me some breathing room."

Nathan and Sister Smith exchanged puzzled glances. "Let's go inside anyway," Nathan said. "It's freezing."

Elder Smith went into an office with three church leaders who were there to greet them, and he discovered one of them was a doctor.

"Could you please take a minute to visit with Marie?" he asked. "She's the young lady who came with us. She's having a hard time."

The doctor went to the foyer where Marie was and invited her and Nathan into a classroom where there was medical equipment.

"I'm Dr. Taylor," he said. "Elder Smith said you haven't been feeling well. Let's see if we can find the cause."

Marie explained to Dr. Taylor how she was feeling, and Nathan couldn't resist chiming in about her actions.

"Nathan, *shut up*," Marie muttered, and the doctor tried to keep a straight face. He checked her vital signs and then gave her a cup.

"Please go to the restroom and provide a urine sample," he said. Marie left and returned before the men really had a chance to talk. Dr. Taylor took the cup from her and tested it with a stick for a minute while Nathan and Marie waited in silence.

"Hmm," Dr. Taylor said. "Well, this should be curable in a few months."

"Oh no, I don't want to be sick that long," Marie said, shaking her head. "Do I have mono?"

"No. Even better. You're pregnant."

Nathan felt like he'd been slapped across the face. He glanced at Marie, and she was frozen in place. But then he swept her into his arms and held her tight.

"I can't believe it," Marie said. "What are we going to do?"

Nathan laughed. "We're going to celebrate."

He shook Dr. Taylor's hand, and they went back to the foyer.

"Did you find out what was wrong?" Sister Smith asked.

"Nothing's wrong," Marie said with a smile. "We're going to have a baby."

Elder Smith let out a whoop. "This is wonderful news! With everything going crazy in the world, this brings it all back to what really matters. Congratulations!"

❧

The next morning the same routine was followed as the Fosters and the Smiths left Star Valley. The plan was to follow the snow plow north into Idaho and skirt along Palisades Reservoir before going directly to the city of Rigby.

This would allow them to bypass the dangerous uprisings that had taken place in Idaho Falls after news spread about the Coalition invasion. The foreign troops were still in California and Oregon, but citizens across the nation were already panicking.

The leaders in Afton had been able to use the ZOOM network to contact the leaders in Rigby, and they told them to be on the lookout for Elder Smith in a few hours.

Marie felt much better after a good night's sleep, and her entire attitude changed now that she knew the cause of her discomfort.

The first part of the trip again went smoothly, but as they drove along the edge of Palisades Reservoir at around noon, the dreaded dark clouds began to build in the western sky. It appeared as if a gray curtain had dropped over the nearby mountains, and large snow flakes began to drift to the ground.

"This isn't looking good," Nathan said. "What if we get stuck out here?"

"The leaders in Rigby were told to expect us by early afternoon," Elder Smith said. "If we don't show up, I expect they'll come searching for us."

During the next half-hour they made better progress than Nathan thought they would, passing through Swan Valley, but soon the weather turned into white-out conditions. The snowplow driver simply stopped in the middle of the road. Nathan had no choice but to stop as well.

"No! We're so close," Elder Smith said. "I've been on this road many times, and we can't be more than twenty miles from Rigby."

"I can't blame him for stopping," Nathan said. "This weather is horrible."

Nathan was nearly ready to get out and talk to the other driver when they saw several sets of lights approaching them. The lights seem to dance up and down.

"What are they?" Marie asked.

"I think they're headlights," Nathan said. "I don't know who would be crazy enough to be out here, but we'll soon find out."

Within five minutes a pack of ten snowmobiles stopped in front of the snowplow, and two men approached their truck. Nathan rolled down the window halfway as one of them lifted his goggles and adjusted his ski mask so he could talk.

"Welcome to Idaho," the man said, looking into the truck. "Is Elder Smith with you?"

"I am," Elder Smith said from the back seat. "Is that my old friend Christopher?"

"Yes! We're here to rescue you!"

"How did you get here so fast?" Elder Smith asked.

"We knew you were driving this route to Rigby, but the storm hit us from the northwest about an hour ago," Christopher said. "So we knew you'd be right in the path of the storm. We figured we'd save us all some trouble and get to you while we could."

"What a blessing," Sister Smith said.

"We've got some winter gear for each of you to put on for the first leg of our journey," Christopher said. "Then in Rigby we've got a Sno-Cat waiting to take you to Rexburg."

CHAPTER 26

Three hours later the Sno-Cat made its way up the hill toward the gleaming Rexburg Temple. The storm had passed, and the windows of the buildings on the BYU-Idaho campus reflected the setting sun.

"Take us to the BYU-Idaho Center," Elder Smith told the driver.

The Sno-Cat turned left onto Center Street and made its way to the middle of campus. Several young adults were shoveling the sidewalks and tidying up entrances to the buildings.

"Is school still in session?" Marie asked.

"Classes continued here on a limited basis for a while," Elder Smith said, "but after the invasion all classwork was suspended. The students were asked to devote their time to helping store the harvested crops. They also assisted in preparing the city for the influx of refugees who will be coming here."

The Sno-Cat stopped on the south side of the BYU-Idaho Center, and the Smiths and Fosters got out. Nathan had heard about this building before, and he was eager to see it. They stepped inside the cavernous lobby.

"Sister Smith and I are going to meet with the other brethren to see what our next options are," Elder Smith said. "Feel free to look around."

Nathan and Marie ascended a large staircase and then opened a door to the balcony of the main auditorium. Marie stepped inside and was in awe. "Wow, this looks just like the Conference Center in Salt Lake! It's so big!"

Nathan gazed across the thousands of seats. "It's actually just a little smaller than the Conference Center, but President Hinckley wanted this building to have the same majestic feeling. With all of the destruction and trouble in Salt Lake, this building will now be the place from where the Church leaders speak to the world."

They lingered for a few minutes in the auditorium, soaking in the special spirit that filled the room. Finally Nathan said, "Let's go check out the basketball courts attached to the building."

"Basketball courts?" Marie asked.

"Yes. There's a large multi-purpose room attached to this building that has ten basketball courts. I'll bet it is being used for something else, though."

They descended the north staircase and entered a hallway to the east where they could see the massive room. Dozens of people were stacking boxes of food and putting cots against the walls. Marie was a little perplexed by all of the activity.

"Maybe I'm missing something," she said, "but Elder Smith mentioned refugees coming here. Who was he talking about?"

"There are still thousands of good Saints who will come here in the next few weeks from the Northwest as they try to escape the Coalition armies. They've been in smaller camps like the people who are gathering to Manti and Logan. They just have a lot farther to travel."

As they watched the flurry of activity, a woman with long brown hair approached them. "Are you the Fosters?" she asked.

"We are," Nathan said. "How can we help you?"

"My name is Sonia, and Elder Smith said I should help you use the ZOOM system to contact your families."

"That would be wonderful," Marie said.

Sonia led them to a room filled with electronic equipment. "We can reach any church facility or camp from this room," she said. "We should be able to chat with them face-to-face. Elder Smith said they were at the Heber Valley Camp. Is that correct?"

"That's where we last saw them," Nathan said. "That would be the first place to check."

Sonia initiated the call, and within a minute they were talking with Elder Cluff.

"Hello!" he said. "You two are now in Rexburg? I can't wait to hear about your journey there. But I think you'll be excited to hear my news. Both of your fathers are here in the camp."

Nathan wasn't sure he had heard him right. "What do you mean? My father died in California, didn't he?"

"Not exactly," Elder Cluff said. "I assure you that both Aaron and Garrett are here with us." He turned to someone and told them to go get Nathan and Marie's families.

As they waited, Elder Cluff excitedly told them about how Garrett had been raised from the dead.

Nathan felt tears come to his eyes. "I still can hardly believe what you're saying."

Just then Garrett's face appeared on the screen. "Hey, son! This is incredible! You both look great."

"I don't know about that," Marie said. "We have some news too, but I want my mom to hear it first."

"She just came through the door," Garrett said. "Here she is."

As Carol's face appeared on the screen, Marie couldn't wait any longer. "Mom, you're going to be a grandma. I'm about two months along."

Carol let out an excited shriek. "I'm so happy for you! Oh, we miss you so much."

They all chatted for another twenty minutes before reluctantly ending the conversation, unsure when they would see each other again. Elder Cluff closed the chat by saying, "We'll be in touch. Please let us know of any developments there."

Sonia led them out of the room and said, "Elder Smith wanted you to join them for dinner when you were finished. I'll take you there now."

They left the BYU-Idaho Center and crossed the plaza to the Manwaring Student Center where a room had been set up for them. The Smiths were already eating, but they stood and welcomed them.

"Were you able to speak with your families?" Sister Smith asked.

"Yes, it was wonderful," Marie said. "My mom kind of freaked out when I told her I was pregnant."

"Mothers will do that," Sister Smith said with a smile.

"The crazy thing is that both of our fathers are now at Heber Valley Camp," Nathan said. He then explained how Garrett and Aaron had been reunited in Copperton, then how Garrett had been shot, but had been brought back from the dead.

"Miracles are happening all around us," Marie said. "I'm so happy they are okay."

Elder Smith was deep in thought as Nathan finished his story. Finally he said, "The meeting I just attended with the other apostles dealt with organizing our defenses against the Coalition forces. We need to intercept their communication transmissions. Aaron's knowledge of the NSA system is invaluable, and Garrett's understanding of the U.N. and Coalition procedures are essential to our plans. We need both of them here now."

"I agree," Nathan said. "But how can we get them here? Look how long it took us to get here, and now with winter setting in and the Coalition attack underway, I just don't see it happening."

Elder Smith didn't respond, instead stabbing a piece of potato and putting it into his mouth. The others began talking among themselves. Nathan thought about what the apostle said, but after what he had just experienced the past week, it just seemed impossible to bring the others to Rexburg.

Suddenly Elder Smith slammed his fist down on the table. "That's it! We'll fly them here."

Everyone at the table went silent. "Are you sure?" Nathan finally asked. "Those jets from Hill Air Force Base would shoot them down without a second thought."

Elder Smith frowned. "I know it's terribly risky, but it must be done. Nathan, once you're finished with your meal, we're getting to work."

Soon the two men kissed their wives good-bye and returned

with Sonia to the BYU-Idaho Center. She helped them reconnect with Elder Cluff at the Heber Valley Camp.

Elder Smith explained his idea to his fellow leader, but Elder Cluff was even more skeptical than Nathan had been.

"We have about a foot of snow covering everything," Elder Cluff said. "How are you going to land a plane here?"

Elder Smith bristled a little. "I know it sounds crazy, but we need those two here for the security of the Church. We can't wait until spring."

Elder Cluff finally relented. "The Heber Airport is a mess, but I'll get my best guys down there to see if we can clear off a runway for you. We got some four-wheelers with plows. Maybe they can get it done."

"Thank you," Elder Smith said. "We'll be in touch after we talk to the airport here."

Nathan tapped him on the shoulder. "Can we have Carol and Denise come too? Marie could really use the support."

Elder Smith nodded and turned back to the screen. "Did you hear that? Send the whole family."

Elder Cluff smiled tiredly. "We'll get them ready. Talk to you soon."

CHAPTER 27

An hour later Elder Smith and Nathan were standing alongside a small eight-seat Cessna jet at the Rexburg Airport. A pilot named Mike Cooper was a friend of Elder Smith's, and after some hesitation, he agreed to fly Nathan to Heber.

"Just to double-check, you really feel we can pull this off?" Mike asked Elder Smith.

"I do. The Lord's hand will guide you."

"I sure hope so," Mike said. "I haven't flown without lights in a long time."

The apostle gave a small grin. "Trust your instruments and you'll be fine."

Mike and Nathan boarded the jet, and soon they were on their way to Utah. They made some small talk. Nathan shared some of his experiences as a maintenance missionary, and Mike told how he had piloted several of the General Authorities to private locations during the past couple of months.

"So I should be getting used to these kinds of adventures, but every time I get nervous," Mike said.

"That's understandable," Nathan replied. "Even with all the evidence that the prophecies are coming true, I keep wondering how I personally fit into the big picture."

It was now completely dark, and Mike kept his eyes glued to the instrument panel. They crossed into Utah and skirted along the eastern edge of the Cache Valley. The spot where Logan should have been looked like an empty valley.

"That's really strange," Nathan said in a panicked voice. "I was in Logan just a few days ago and it was a thriving community. What happened to it?"

Mike chuckled. "I would've thought you'd know the answer to that. The Lord has hidden it from view. There's some sort of spiritual shield that covers the Places of Refuge. Otherwise, the government would bomb the tarnation out of them."

"So you've seen this before?" Nathan asked.

"Yes, I had to fly an apostle and his wife to the Place of Refuge near Hurricane, Utah, and I honestly couldn't see it until the apostle asked the Lord to take the veil from my eyes. Then suddenly there it was—the whole city filled with tents. Hundreds of people were moving around, where just moments before it looked like a valley filled with sand and sagebrush."

"That's marvelous," Nathan said. "I'm going to try it."

He then prayed aloud for a glimpse of Logan, and when he looked down again, he could see rows of lights and several bonfires.

"I see it! It's there!"

Then the scene vanished and everything was dark again.

Nathan shook his head in wonderment. "It's gone now, but the Lord answered my prayer. Incredible!"

Within minutes the instruments showed they were above Park City, but everything felt strange. They couldn't see a thing, other than the faint outline of Mount Timpanogos to the right.

"I feel we're too low," Mike said. "The instruments seem wrong."

Just then they saw a campfire on a hill *above* them.

"Whoa, we're in trouble!" Mike said.

"Trust in the Lord," Nathan said. "Take your hands off the controls."

"No way," Mike said. "Are you nuts?"

"Do it or we're going to die!"

Mike closed his eyes and lifted his hands. The plane suddenly swerved upward to the left, and they could feel a multitude of tree tops scraping the bottom of the plane. Once the plane leveled out, Mike put his hands back on the controls.

"Well done, pilot," Nathan said softly. They were both shaken up, but they knew they had witnessed yet another miracle.

Nathan pointed off into the distance. "Hey, can you see that row of flares? That must be the Heber Airport."

❧

Elder Cluff was so tired he could hardly stand as he watched Paul and Jake set out ten flares in a long line down the runway. They had reached the airport without too much trouble, but the runway was covered with debris from the flood.

Paul and Jake had tried to clear off as much of the junk as they could with the plows of the four-wheelers, but some of the logs and rocks were just too heavy.

Aaron, Garrett, Carol and Denise had then joined Elder Cluff in helping clean off the runway by hand while Paul and Jake kept clearing the snow the best they could. It was exhausting and they were all muddy, but the runway was now clear.

As they paused to rest, Denise could hear the faint sound of an airplane.

"Quiet!" she called out. "Can you hear that?"

Just then the plane briefly turned its lights on, and the group let out a cheer.

"They made it," Carol said happily.

The plane touched down and rolled to a stop within five feet of the final stretch where they had cleared the snow.

While Mike stayed in the plane, Nathan hopped out and was surrounded by his loved ones. Garrett gave him a big hug, followed by Denise and Carol. Even Aaron gave him a big bear hug.

They then stepped back and wiped away their tears of joy as Elder Cluff, Paul, and Jake shook Nathan's hand.

"So you had a smooth trip?" Elder Cluff asked him.

"Well, no, but the Lord watched out for us. Let's hope he can do that one more time on the way back."

Then things got emotional for another minute as everyone bid farewell to the three men who would be staying behind.

Aaron started crying as he grasped Paul by the arm. "Time and again you and Jake have rescued our family," he said. "We'll never forget you."

Everyone else shared their thanks with them as well, and then they boarded the jet. The plane shuddered as they took off, and for a moment it felt like they might not get enough altitude, but Garrett called out above the engine noise, "We'll be all right. I'm not going to die twice in a week."

That comment broke the tension. They zoomed into the air and turned north toward Rexburg.

Garrett gave Nathan a high five. "Rexburg, here we come!"

❧

Mike landed the plane at the Rexburg Airport in the wee hours of the morning. He'd been nervously watching the fuel gauge, but the needle had stayed at an eighth of a tank for the past hour.

"Just another tender mercy," he said as he pulled the plane over to a lighted hangar.

Sonia was there waiting for them, and once everyone was safely off the plane and in the hanger, she explained Marie had felt ill again.

"Marie asked to be taken to a home in northern Rexburg," Sonia said. "She said one of your relatives lives there."

"That must be my cousin Mark," Carol said. "In all of the commotion of the past few hours I'd forgotten he and his family were up here."

"They are eager to accommodate you," Sonia said. "That will be our first stop."

They started loading into a van, but Nathan took a moment to find Mike.

"We can't thank you enough for helping us out," Nathan said.

"No problem," Mike said. "You've got a special family."

❧

A few minutes later, the van pulled into the driveway of a medium-sized, red-brick home. The front door opened, and Marie stood there under the porch light. Carol and Aaron could hardly get the van doors open fast enough. They hurried to her side and embraced her.

"I've missed you both so much," she told them. "This is like a very wonderful dream."

Soon everyone had gathered in the front room to get out of the cold, and as everyone was chatting about the past day's events, Aaron smiled at his daughter. He said, "I need to apologize for trying to stop you from taking that internship in Chicago."

"What do you mean?" Marie asked.

Aaron shrugged. "When you left, we were sure it was going to be a disaster."

Marie tilted her head. "Well, wasn't it?"

"Not at all. I'd say it was a success. Because of that internship, you're happily married in the temple and have a baby on the way. That's all your mom and I ever wanted."

Marie rolled her eyes and playfully punched her dad in the arm. She said, "I know you're dying to tell me 'I told you so,' but I wouldn't change a thing of how this all came together."

Aaron suddenly got misty-eyed and gave her a hug. He whispered in her ear, "You know what? Neither would I."

CHAPTER 28

The family spent the next couple of days getting organized at Mark's home in northern Rexburg. There was plenty of room in the house, but Mark had also stockpiled several large tents that could be set up in the nearby field. He had plenty of provisions, a solar generator to provide electricity, and a deep well that supplied pure spring water. They all agreed the home would serve nicely as a gathering place for their extended family.

Marie was in the midst of steady bouts of morning sickness, so she was especially grateful for two fully functioning bathrooms to make the experience slightly more bearable.

Three days after their arrival, Aaron and Garrett were helping set up five big tents in the field behind the home. The snow from the storm had melted off, and they felt it would be a good time to get the tents ready before another storm hit.

While they were working in the field, a black sedan pulled into the driveway behind the house. It was followed by the same van that had brought them from the airport.

Elder Smith stepped out of the sedan, and both men called out to him. He waved and came over to the tent they had set up.

"Do you think it will hold up through the winter?" Elder Smith asked as he tugged on the canvas.

"I hope so," Aaron said. "Carol keeps hinting that this is where the men are going to be sleeping."

"She might not be joking," Elder Smith said.

He then turned and pointed back toward the vehicles.

"I want you to keep this van," Elder Smith said. "You both have valuable knowledge about our enemies, and there will be times when we'll need you to come meet with us. We'll show you where the Church's gasoline supply is, and you can fill up the van when needed."

"That's very kind," Garrett said. "I wasn't looking forward to the walk into town."

"There's also another reason I'm visiting you today," Elder Smith said. "Your family is invited to a special meeting tomorrow evening in the BYU-Idaho Center. The prophet has finally arrived here after visiting most of the larger camps, and they are going to broadcast the meeting on the ZOOM network to all of the Saints."

"I can't wait," Aaron said. "I'll go tell the others."

The man who had driven the van was now in the sedan, ready to take the apostle back to Rexburg. Elder Smith started to get in the car, but he looked at Garrett and said, "I sense that you have a question for me."

Garrett kicked at the ground. "I do, but I don't quite know how to ask it."

Elder Smith put his hand on his shoulder. "Go ahead. Ask me anything you want."

"Well, you might know a little bit about my background, but let's just say I've made some bad choices. I'm currently an excommunicated member of the Church. I actually have two wives who have passed away. I don't know how that's going to work out, but right now I'm not worthy to be with them, and it hurts. I want to get back on track. Can you help me?"

Elder Smith nodded. "When you were in the Spirit World, did you have a life review?"

"Yes. It was excruciating."

"Why?"

Garrett paused and frowned. "I suppose it was because I realized the only thing that mattered in life was my family, particularly

Nathan and Denise, as well as my relationship with the Savior. I had been focused on other things."

"Do you remember the story of Alma the Younger in the Book of Mormon?" Elder Smith asked.

"Certainly," Garrett said. "I know exactly how he felt."

"From my observation, you've had a similar change of heart," Elder Smith said. "Is that true?"

"I have. I want to be rebaptized and hold the priesthood again. How long do you think it will take?"

"Well, I'll talk to the First Presidency about it as soon as I have the opportunity," Elder Smith said.

"Thank you so much," Garrett said, wiping away a tear.

"You're a good man," the apostle said. "The Lord is happy that you want to come back. We need you."

⁊

The next evening, the Shaw and Foster clan made their way to their seats in the BYU-Idaho Center. Elder Smith had reserved spots for them near the front of the auditorium next to Sister Smith, and he waved to them from his chair on the stand.

Nathan marveled at the scene. The Tabernacle Choir was in position facing them, along with a good portion of the General Authorities. If he didn't know any better, he would have thought he was in the Conference Center in Salt Lake City.

Then a door opened, and the prophet of the Lord stepped into the room. Everyone instinctively rose to their feet. He looked at the capacity crowd of 15,000 Saints and smiled widely.

Then a lone deep male voice in the Choir began singing the following song:

We thank thee, O God, for a prophet
To guide us in these latter days.
We thank thee for sending the gospel
To lighten our minds with its rays.

The Spirit was so strong that people were openly weeping. The prophet smiled again and said loudly, "Everyone join in."

So the Choir and the congregation began again. The choir's accompanist hurried to the organ and played along.

We thank thee for every blessing
Bestowed by thy bounteous hand.
We feel it a pleasure to serve thee
And love to obey thy command.

When dark clouds of trouble hang o'er us
And threaten our peace to destroy,
There is hope smiling brightly before us,
And we know that deliv'rance is nigh.

At this point, Garrett couldn't sing another word. His heart was so filled with gratitude that he felt it might burst.

We doubt not the Lord nor his goodness.
We've proved him in days that are past.
The wicked who fight against Zion
Will surely be smitten at last.

We'll sing of his goodness and mercy.
We'll praise him by day and by night,
Rejoice in his glorious gospel,
And bask in its life-giving light.

Thus on to eternal perfection
The honest and faithful will go,
While they who reject this glad message
Shall never such happiness know.

As the final note echoed away, the prophet made his way to the pulpit. "Thank you," he said. "That wasn't a planned part of the program, but I'm sure the Lord is pleased with it."

The prophet turned to the Choir and said, "I appreciate the vocal solo that got us going. That was perfect."

He then sat down and the congregation took their seats again as well. One of the counselors in the First Presidency went to the podium to conduct the meeting.

"Welcome to this special broadcast," he said. "Through the ZOOM network, thousands of members throughout the world are joining us at this time. Whether you are in a church building or in a tent on a high mountaintop, please know that we love you and appreciate your faithfulness in following the word of the Lord."

The Choir then sang an opening song, "Our Savior's Love," followed by an opening prayer.

The counselor then returned to the pulpit and said, "As many of you know, we have lost some of our dear apostles during the past few months. Those vacancies have been filled, and I will now read the names of the reorganized First Presidency and Quorum of the Twelve Apostles for your sustaining vote."

Everyone listened carefully, and as the names of the new apostles were read, there were a few gasps of delight at the additions to the quorum. They were youthful men who were already fairly well-known in the Church and who would serve diligently and inspire the Saints. The sustaining vote was unanimous, and the newly called brethren took their places on the stand.

Then the prophet stood again at the pulpit and smiled happily at the congregation. His grin was infectious and made the Saints feel that even if the world was crashing down, the prophet wasn't going to let it affect his positive outlook on life.

"Let me begin by saying you are exactly where the Lord wants you to be," he said. "The past few months have been a challenge for each one of us, but you are on the path to a great eternal reward. Much like our Pioneer predecessors, we are being refined and polished. They endured much to become a better people—a people that could take a dry desert and make it blossom like the rose.

"It is now our turn to be polished and prepared for the next great step in the Lord's plan for his Saints. We are becoming a Zion people, casting aside our worldly desires and becoming one as we help each other. As we become united, our spiritual unity will become manifest as we soon build the New Jerusalem and other Cities of Light across this land.

"But the time is not yet. As you know, North America is under attack by foreign invaders. Some of our greatest cities now lay in ruins, and millions of our fellow citizens have lost their lives. It is a dark time.

"Downtown Salt Lake is under siege right now by U.N. forces. Temple Square and our other Church buildings are surrounded by enemy troops. They feel they've stopped us, but that isn't true. The Lord is always several steps ahead of the adversary.

"When Martin Harris lost the 116 pages of the original Book of Mormon manuscript, the Lord had foreknowledge of that event. He had inspired the prophet Mormon many centuries earlier to include other plates for Joseph Smith to translate that covered the same information that was lost.

"In a similar way, the Lord has prepared ahead for today's troubles. He knew Salt Lake would suffer calamities, and so over the past few years he has inspired his prophets to quietly construct this particular building, the BYU-Idaho Center, to thwart the enemy and still have a place from where the voices of the prophet and apostles can be heard across the world."

"Many of you listening to this broadcast may never have even heard of the BYU-Idaho Center. Under President Gordon B. Hinckley's inspired direction, this magnificent structure was completed and dedicated in 2010.

"I want to share a statement given by Elder David A. Bednar at the dedication of this building. He said:

"I never cease to stand all amazed at the miracle the Lord has enacted and continues to bring forth at Brigham Young University–Idaho. At this pulpit as I look over this large congregation and into your faces, it is clear to me that this facility has been constructed at this time and in this place for reasons we do not yet fully comprehend or

understand. As 'we wait upon the Lord' (Isaiah 40:31), His purposes will be revealed and accomplished—and you and I will declare that indeed The Lord is able to do His own work. This dedicatory service today truly is historic, and you will one day tell your children and grandchildren that you were present when this remarkable facility was dedicated."

The prophet then spoke for several minutes about his recent visits to several camps throughout the Rocky Mountains. He shared how powerful miracles were happening due to the faithfulness of the Saints.

"The sick and afflicted have been healed, and the lame now walk," he said. "There are even some among us who have been raised from the dead."

Garrett nodded gratefully, and his friends and relatives looked down the row at him.

The prophet then shifted gears and spoke of how the Saints were simply doing what the Nephites of old had done during dangerous times.

"Gathering together as Saints in times of danger has always been part of the Lord's plan," the prophet said. "We read in Third Nephi chapter 3 of when the Gadianton Robbers had become so prevalent that the Church leaders in that day had no choice but to do what we have done. The scriptures say:

"*. . . they had taken their horses, and their chariots, and their cattle, and all their flocks, and their herds, and their grain, and all their substance, and did march forth by thousands and by tens of thousands, until they had all gone forth to the place which had been appointed that they should gather themselves together, to defend themselves against their enemies.*"

"So take heart," the prophet said. "You are just the latest generation to have the Lord watching over you."

He then raised his hand and asked, "How many of you still have close friends or relatives who are still in the valleys?"

Nearly every hand in the room went up.

"We have not forgotten them," the prophet said. "They have

been tried and chastened for their slothfulness, but the Lord still loves them. The invading forces have taken over most of the country and have made our task difficult, but we will be organizing rescue efforts to retrieve our loved ones. They still have their agency whether to join us, but over the next few weeks, we hope to bring to safety as many of them as possible."

The prophet then bore a powerful testimony of the Church's destiny before the Second Coming, and the Choir closed by singing, "The Spirit of God," which brought the meeting to a powerful crescendo.

Following the closing prayer, Elder Smith came down from the stand and greeted everyone.

"What an incredible meeting," Marie told him. "It really helped me see the big picture again. Sometimes I forget that."

"Yes, it's so wonderful to have the prophet among us, and those new apostles will bring great vitality and strength to our quorum."

Elder Smith then turned to Aaron. "I wanted to catch you before you left. I need you, Garrett, and Nathan to return here tomorrow morning for a special meeting. Will that work?"

"I'm sure it will," Aaron said. "We'll be here."

"Let's meet here at 10 a.m. in the south lobby. We have a lot to discuss."

CHAPTER 29

The next morning Aaron, Garrett, and Nathan arrived at the BYU-Idaho Center shortly before 10 a.m. They had discussed what the meeting could possibly be about, but no one was really sure.

"Maybe we'll be in charge of a rescue mission," Garrett said.

Nathan shrugged. "Possibly, but I was hoping for a little more time to recuperate from our last adventure."

They spotted Elder Smith coming down the hall, accompanied by two of the newly sustained apostles.

"Whoa," Garrett said. "I feel a little out of place."

The apostles reached them, and they all introduced themselves. Elder Smith then invited the group into a room filled with computers and media equipment.

"First things first. Aaron, welcome to your new office," Elder Smith said. "We've tapped into the NSA computer system, which the United Nations now controls. But you know how it works better than anyone. We need you to help monitor the Coalition's movements and keep us updated on any other developments."

"It will be an honor," Aaron said. One of the new apostles motioned to him, and they went to a cubicle in the far corner of the room where Aaron began to work.

Elder Smith then looked at Nathan. "I remember when you were lying in that hospital bed in Minnesota after you had saved my life. The Spirit bore witness that you still had a great work to perform. You've already accomplished much, but now you and your father are going to help prepare the Elders of Israel to defend their liberty."

Nathan was surprised. "I'm not a soldier."

"No, but you're a natural leader, and the men will follow your example. Throughout the winter we'll be organizing and training the men in the camps to go to war against the Coalition and save our country."

Garrett nodded thoughtfully. "You're talking about the prophecy of the boys coming down from the mountains."

"That's right," Elder Smith said.

Nathan looked confused. "I guess I must have missed that one. What prophecy?"

Garrett smiled. "Hey, I know something you don't! Joseph Smith prophesied that when the United States was on the brink of defeat, the 'boys from the mountains' would rush forth and save the country."

"You're right," Elder Smith said. "The prophet also referred to them as the Elders of Israel. That's the group we are going to organize and train in the coming weeks. Garrett, your knowledge will be invaluable."

Garrett frowned. "How many men will be available to help us? We're not going to defeat the Coalition with what we've got here in Rexburg."

"Don't worry, we'll have men from the camps throughout the West. That's one of the main reasons the Saints have now gathered into larger groups, such as in Logan and Manti. We'll be able to train them better that way, as well as combine them more easily into one unit when the time comes."

"That's very wise," Garrett said. "I know enough about how the Coalition operates that we can exploit their weaknesses."

"Exactly," Elder Smith said. "That's why we couldn't leave you at the Heber Valley Camp all winter."

Just then Aaron called out to them. "Hey, we might already have a situation developing. I've located a fairly large Coalition convoy in Montana traveling south on I-15. Do we have any defenses set up in Idaho Falls?"

They all hurried over to Aaron's cubicle, where he had an

interactive map on the screen that showed the convoy's location."

"The Saints in the southern end of the valley have built a defensive blockade at the overpass in the town of Ucon, but we couldn't stop a full U.N. convoy if they turn onto Highway 20 and come our way. How far away are they?"

"They're just south of Butte, about 200 miles away. They aren't moving very fast, so I bet they'll stop for the night somewhere north of here. But they'll definitely reach Idaho Falls by morning."

"Get me to Idaho Falls," Garrett said. "I can talk to them."

"Surely you aren't going alone," Elder Smith said.

"No, I need some muscle behind me to look authentic. I will create a U.N. uniform for myself, but everyone else can be dressed in U.S. Army gear. You mentioned a group of defenders stationed at the Ucon overpass. Please contact them and tell them to be armed and ready to march to Idaho Falls this evening."

❧

The next morning Nathan and several other men were stationed at Exit 119 on I-15 in Idaho Falls. They had parked several vehicles to block the onramp leading to Rexburg.

Nathan and the other men were dressed in U.S. Army gear and were fully armed. They were stationed in a building near the freeway exit, awaiting Garrett's orders. Nathan peered out of a doorway, looking for his father.

Some of the men worried that they would be seen as enemies, but Garrett planned to tell the Coalition leaders that he had convinced the soldiers to join the Coalition's cause.

Nathan had never actually fired a semi-automatic rifle. He was ready to do so if needed, but he was praying that his father's negotiating skills would spare them a shootout.

He had been surprised at how empty Idaho Falls was. They had seen quite a few people still in the city, but any active LDS members had moved closer to Rexburg, while a large number of non-members had headed elsewhere as word had spread of the

Coalition's attack on the West Coast.

"Heavenly Father, please be with my father," Nathan prayed. "Guide him to say whatever will preserve us."

~

Garrett had spent the morning putting the finishing touches on his U.N. uniform and helmet. It wasn't perfect, but he hoped it would do the job.

"This is crazy," he said to himself. "I might be headed back to the Spirit World sooner than I planned."

His hand-held radio crackled to life as he walked toward a jeep that would take him to meet the Coalition convoy.

"Garrett, are you there?" Aaron's voice echoed from the radio.

"I'm here. Do have any updates?"

"Yes. The lead vehicles of the Convoy are now about a mile from Exit 119. You should begin to see them soon. Good luck."

Garrett got into the jeep and signaled for the driver to drive forward. He had rigged a white pillow case to a pole, and he now held it above him, allowing it to flap in the wind.

Within seconds, Garrett spotted a five-axle transport vehicle rolling toward him.

"Pull into the middle of the road and stop," he told the driver. "Then wait for me."

Once the jeep was stopped, Garrett climbed out and slowly walked toward the Coalition vehicle, waving the white flag above him. The vehicle came to a stop, and an angry voice emanated from the speakers. "Get out of the way or we will crush you."

Garrett kept moving toward the transporter, though, until he was within thirty yards. Then he called out, "I'm with the United Nations. This is my jurisdiction. We need to talk."

After a few seconds, a tall Chinese man in a Coalition uniform stepped out of the transporter, along with another soldier holding a rife that was pointed at Garrett's chest.

Garrett put his hands up. "Hey, I'm unarmed. I just wanted to let you know I captured a group of U.S. soldiers who have sworn allegiance to the Coalition."

"You did not kill them outright?" the leader asked in broken English. "That's what we did in Oregon."

"No. I gave them the option to either die or join us," Garrett said, trying to keep the conversation going without revealing too much information. "They're now on our side, and we've secured the upcoming freeway exit to keep civilians from fleeing."

The Chinese leader seemed unsure of this strange American who was saying all of the right things and didn't seem the least afraid of them. But it still seemed odd for this man to be leading a group of U.N. forces.

"Who is your commanding officer?" he asked. "Is it someone I know?"

"Commander Klopov, of course," Garrett said.

That name struck a chord with the Coalition leader. "Oh, I didn't realize the U.N. forces had come so far north. The last I heard, your soldiers were still in Salt Lake."

Garrett nodded. "Most of our troops are still there, but Commander Klopov wanted me to clamp down on Idaho Falls. Too many people were escaping into the wilderness. We have effectively shut it down, but we didn't have enough manpower to control Pocatello, the next big city to the south. So we really need your help there. Are things under control where you've been?"

The two Chinese soldiers looked at each other and shrugged. "It really hasn't been much of a challenge so far. We feel it's kind of like hunting rabbits. The people run away from you and you knock them down. One time I even got two with one shot."

"That's how it was here," Garrett said. "Nice and easy."

"So everything is taken care of?" the Chinese leader asked, sweeping his arm to the north.

"Yes, there were just a few potato farmers out there who tried to fight us, but we outnumbered them. In fact, things are so slow here I'll probably just leave a few men at this freeway junction and then try to catch up to you."

Suddenly the Chinese leader looked closely at Garrett's face. "You look familiar. Don't I know you from somewhere?"

His fellow soldier said something to him in Chinese, and they both started laughing. Garrett started to sweat a little.

"That's it," the leader said, still chuckling. "You look like the American traitor."

"Me? I'm American, but I'm devoted to the United Nations."

"Haven't you seen the video of him?" he asked.

Garrett shook his head. "I don't know what you're talking about. I would like to see it."

The other soldier went to the transporter and brought back a laptop computer.

"The Coalition wants us to show this video to our soldiers as a reminder of what will happen if they step out of line. This man was part of the U.N. forces, just like you. He tried to escape, but they caught up to him and made him pay."

The video started, and Garrett recognized himself facing the camera. The sound was muffled, but after an verbal exchange with someone off camera, Garrett saw himself crumple to the ground as blood spurted from three bullet holes in his chest.

He looked at the Chinese leader. "That's pretty wild. That guy could be my brother. He got what he deserved, though."

Garrett pointed toward the Coalition convoy. "Well, I'm sure your soldiers are getting antsy, so we'll let you move on through. I'll contact Commander Klopov and tell him you're heading to Pocatello to give us a hand. Just give me a minute to tell my troops to let you through. I'll lead the way."

Garrett returned to the jeep, trying to keep a calm demeanor, although his heart was racing.

"Just drive slowly," he told the driver as he grabbed a megaphone from the back seat. As the jeep approached Exit 119, he shouted, "Soldiers, come to the side of the road. Hold your weapons at your side as the Coalition convoy passes by. Don't move a muscle until they are past us."

❧

Nathan heard his father's command and hurried to join his fellow soldiers in lining the freeway. There were about fifty Elders of Israel on each side of the pavement as the Coalition transporters and tanks rumbled by. Some of the Coalition soldiers waved at them, and Nathan couldn't help but give a slight nod back.

The Elders of Israel stood in place until the convoy was in the distance and Garrett's jeep circled back to them. He pointed toward the overpass, and everyone hurried up to the top of it, where they watched the convoy continue down I-15 for several miles toward Pocatello.

Nathan went to his father's side. "I'm not sure what you said, but it worked," he said.

"The Lord put words in my mouth," Garrett said. "They should have figured me out, but we'll take what we can get. It buys us some time to get better prepared. That one convoy had more firepower than we have. If they had turned and gone to Rexburg, everything might have been lost."

CHAPTER 30

The Elders of Israel returned to the defense line at the Ucon overpass, and word quickly spread throughout Rigby, Rexburg, and the other towns of Garrett's successful tactics in dealing with the Coalition convoy. It sparked a sense of patriotic fervor among the Saints, and the prophet knew it was important to capitalize on it immediately.

A meeting was called for the following evening at the BYU-Idaho Center. Every male over the age of 18 was urged to attend. Garrett had been invited to speak, and Nathan sat on the stand with him.

Garrett spoke first, and he had everyone on the edge of their seats with his rousing account of facing the leader of the Coalition convoy. He closed by saying, "I assure you they can be defeated. They are simply mortal men like us. They have big machines, but we have the Lord on our side. The power of men cannot match the power of God. You are the Lord's modern-day warriors. I salute you!"

The prophet then spoke. "I don't foresee us going to battle until the spring," he said. "The invading army is still strong and will continue to cleanse this nation throughout the winter. But by spring they will be weakened, and that is when we will be our strongest."

He then outlined a physical fitness regimen that each man would be required to participate in.

"If you discover that you just can't do it, particularly the older men, we will find other ways for you to serve. But I urge each of you to get into the best shape of your life. We will outperform the enemy in every way. If we are physically superior, we are much more likely to prevail.

"It is also important for each of you to receive the Melchizedek Priesthood and receive your temple endowment. This will clothe you with the full armor of God, and you will be fully prepared to face the spiritual challenges that come in warfare."

He then paused and opened a set of scriptures. "For many years, members of the Church have speculated why there are so many chapters in the Book or Mormon about wars. I testify that they were included as a blueprint for us to use. The time has come for us to learn from them and implement them as we defend ourselves.

"I have recently heard of some young men that are saddened that they haven't been able to serve a standard proselyting mission like their fathers and older brothers did. But I assure you this is a full-time mission, and at the proper time you will each be set apart in this calling.

"You are the modern equivalent of Helaman's 2,000 stripling warriors. You have been raised by your parents as righteous young men who are willing to defend their homes and families."

The prophet then thrust his right arm into the air and called out, "I now ask you what Helaman asked those young men: 'Therefore what say ye, my sons, will ye go against them to battle?'"

A shout rose up from the thousands of young men in the BYU-Idaho Center.

"We will!"

The prophet thrust both arms in the air and joined with them as they shouted a second time, "We will!"

"Thank you, my beloved brethren. You are a chosen generation. It is time to reclaim our liberty!"

❧

After the meeting, the prophet took Garrett by the arm and said, "Elder Smith talked to me yesterday, and the Lord has approved your request for rebaptism. Am I right in guessing you would like this fine son of yours to perform the ordinance?"

"Absolutely," Garrett said, smiling at Nathan."

"Wonderful," the prophet said. "I will notify your stake president and bishop. Please move forward with the baptism and confirmation in the next couple of days, then we'll discuss restoring all of your priesthood and temple blessings. We need you to be at full spiritual power as you lead us forward."

The following Sunday a crowd of about twenty people gathered around the small pond on Mark's property. A hose attached to the well had been running steadily into the pond ever since they had returned from the meeting in Rexburg, and now the pond glistened with pure spring water.

Nathan and Garrett were dressed in white, and they stepped out into the pond.

"Thank you for all of your support," Garrett said to the crowd. "I feel so blessed to be among you."

Nathan then took his father's wrist with his left hand and raised his right arm to the square. He fought off the tears long enough to say, "Garrett Foster, having been commissioned of Jesus Christ, I baptize you in the name of the Father, and of the Son, and of the Holy Ghost. Amen."

Nathan then lowered Garrett backward into the water until he was completely submerged, then pulled him up again. They gave a quick embrace, then worked their way to the pond bank.

Denise was waiting there with towels for both of them.

"Nathan, that's pretty impressive," Aaron said as he helped them out of the water. "You baptized your father and your sister in the same year."

"And both times the water was freezing cold!" Nathan said playfully. "But I wouldn't change a thing."

Garrett had asked Aaron to confirm him a member of the

Church, and so after the men had changed clothes, everyone gathered inside the house for the confirmation. Then the women got busy dishing up a delicious meal with plenty of desserts.

Aaron spotted Garrett piling his plate high and then adding a piece of chocolate cake on the side.

"Hey, soldier," Aaron said harshly. "Aren't you going to watch your diet?"

Garrett gave him a wink. "Training doesn't start until next week."

Nathan stood in the corner with his arms around Marie as they watched their fathers banter back and forth.

"You're a good man, Nathan," she said, hugging him tight. "None of this would have happened without you."

Nathan stayed silent. He was humbled that she would say that. He had simply sought to follow the Lord.

He vowed to cherish this brief time with his family in Rexburg. It was a miracle that they were all together, but deep down he knew it was only temporary. He sensed there were people in that room who would soon give their lives for the gospel. It hurt to contemplate, but he knew it would be for the glory of God.

"I'm ready, Lord," he thought. "Bring it on."

Preparing for Battle

As winter descended on the Rocky Mountains and the snow piled up, the Places of Refuge became more isolated from the rest of the nation. Rexburg became a forgotten place in the minds of the Coalition leaders as their armies surged toward the center of the country from both coasts.

During this time, Garrett spearheaded an extensive training program for the Elders of Israel. Supplies were moved out of the multi-use area of the BYU-Idaho Center, and that huge gymnasium became a beehive of athletic activity. The various training sessions were videotaped and sent out via the ZOOM network to other gathering places so that the men in those camps could implement the information and be prepared as well.

Weapons and ammunition stockpiles were gathered in from members' homes and catalogued. Then those Saints who were skilled in creating guns and swords were put to work creating additional ones.

In addition to helping Garrett, Nathan and Marie were assigned by Elder Smith to a committee that created a new daily gospel curriculum for all families. It focused on the words of the prophets in the last days and on preparing for the Second Coming of Jesus Christ. Thanks to the lessons, many topics that were considered frightening or "too deep" just a year or two earlier were now eagerly and openly discussed among the Saints on a daily basis.

Meanwhile, Carol and Denise were fully occupied in helping keep everyone fed and clothed. One entire building on the BYU-Idaho campus was devoted to making clothing.

Refugees from the Northwest began arriving, and they were treated kindly. Many families pitched their tents in Rexburg, while others were welcomed by Saints in communities all the way south to Rigby.

There was a spirit of unity that had never been equaled among the Saints. In some ways it was easy to forget a war was going on just a few hundred miles away.

But Aaron never forgot. He spent hours each day tracking the Coalition forces, then reporting the latest developments to the First Presidency. They watched from afar as Denver, Colorado was established as the new Coalition headquarters.

The United States was on the brink of being completely conquered, but there were still a few pockets of rebellion in the Midwest. Otherwise, the Coalition would have declared complete victory. Instead, they were content to wait out the harsh winter, and then annihilate their remaining opponents.

Little did they know what the Elders of Israel would be bringing their way in the spring.

Join the Saints in their quest for freedom when the *Times of Turmoil* series continues in *Book Four: Reclaiming Liberty.*

About the Author

Chad Daybell has worked in the publishing business for the past two decades and has written more than 25 books.

The *Times of Turmoil* series is a sequel to Chad's bestselling *Standing in Holy Places* series, which continues to find success in both the LDS bookstores and the national retail chains.

Chad is also known for his other novels such as *Chasing Paradise* and *The Emma Trilogy*, as well as his non-fiction books for youth, including *The Aaronic Priesthood* and *The Youth of Zion*. He and his wife Tammy also created the *Tiny Talks* series for Primary children.

He is currently the president of Spring Creek Book Company. Visit **www.springcreekbooks.com** to see the company's lineup of titles.

Learn about Chad at his personal website **www.cdaybell.com** where he regularly blogs about his books and experiences.